FIRST LABEL
—BOOK ONE—

BRIX'S
Bid

USA TODAY BESTSELLING AUTHOR
HEATHER SLADE

BRIX'S BID

© 2022 Heather Slade

All rights reserved. No part of this book may be used or reproduced in any manner whatsoever without written permission, except in the case of brief quotations embodied in critical articles and reviews.

This book is a work of fiction. The names, characters, places and incidents are products of the writer's imagination or have been used fictitiously and are not to be construed as real. Any resemblance to persons, living or dead, actual events, locale or organizations is entirely coincidental.

979-8-88649-317-7

MORE FROM AUTHOR HEATHER SLADE

BUTLER RANCH
Kade's Worth
Brodie's Promise
Maddox's Truce
Naughton's Secret
Mercer's Vow
Kade's Return
Butler Ranch Christmas

WICKED WINEMAKERS
FIRST LABEL
Brix's Bid
Ridge's Release
Press' Passion
Zin's Sins
Tryst's Temptation

WICKED WINEMAKERS
SECOND LABEL
Beau's Beloved
Coming Soon:
Cru's Crush
Bones' Bliss
Snapper's Seduction
Kick's Kiss

ROARING FORK RANCH
Coming Soon:
Roaring Fork Wrangler
Roaring Fork Roughstock
Roaring Fork Rockstar
Roaring Fork Rooker
Roaring Fork Bridger

THE ROYAL AGENTS
OF MI6
Make Me Shiver
Drive Me Wilder
Feel My Pinch
Chase My Shadow
Find My Angel

K19 SECURITY
SOLUTIONS TEAM ONE
Razor's Edge
Gunner's Redemption
Mistletoe's Magic
Mantis' Desire
Dutch's Salvation

K19 SECURITY
SOLUTIONS TEAM TWO
Striker's Choice
Monk's Fire
Halo's Oath
Tackle's Honor
Onyx's Awakening

K19 SHADOW OPERATIONS
TEAM ONE
Code Name: Ranger
Code Name: Diesel
Code Name: Wasp
Code Name: Cowboy
Code Name: Mayhem

K19 ALLIED INTELLIGENCE
TEAM ONE
Code Name: Ares
Code Name: Cayman
Code Name: Poseidon
Code Name: Zeppelin
Code Name: Magnet

K19 ALLIED INTELLIGENCE
TEAM TWO
Code Name: Puck
Code Name: Michelangelo
Coming Soon:
Code Name: Typhon
Code Name: Hornet
Code Name: Reaper

PROTECTORS
UNDERCOVER
Undercover Agent
Undercover Emissary
Coming Soon:
Undercover Savior
Undercover Infidel
Undercover Assassin

THE INVINCIBLES
TEAM ONE
Code Name: Deck
Code Name: Edge
Code Name: Grinder
Code Name: Rile
Code Name: Smoke

THE INVINCIBLES
TEAM TWO
Code Name: Buck
Code Name: Irish
Code Name: Saint
Code Name: Hammer
Code Name: Rip

THE UNSTOPPABLES
TEAM ONE
Code Name: Fury
Code Name: Married

COWBOYS OF
CRESTED BUTTE
A Cowboy Falls
A Cowboy's Dance
A Cowboy's Kiss
A Cowboy Stays
A Cowboy Wins

Table of Contents

Prologue 1
Chapter 1 3
Chapter 2 15
Chapter 3 33
Chapter 4 45
Chapter 5 54
Chapter 6 62
Chapter 7 70
Chapter 8 84
Chapter 9 95
Chapter 10 111
Chapter 11 125
Chapter 12 135
Chapter 13 145
Chapter 14 159
Chapter 15 168
Chapter 16 180
Chapter 17 194
Chapter 18 210
Chapter 19 216

Chapter 20 219
Chapter 21 226
Chapter 22 237
Chapter 23 244
Chapter 24 255
Chapter 25 261
Chapter 26 267
Chapter 27 277
Chapter 28 294
Chapter 29 296
Chapter 30 310
Chapter 31 327
Chapter 32 337
Chapter 33 342
Epilogue 349
Ridge's Release 355
About the Author 357

Prologue

Brix

"One of our own is in trouble."

After my blunt statement, the wine cellar grew eerily quiet. Every one of the men of Los Caballeros Society—not named for my family's winery as everyone assumed, but rather the other way around—moved closer to the table.

The secret society dating back to our grandfathers' grandfathers only met when necessary, when someone needed our help. We were brothers—some by blood, some not, but brothers all the same.

"Who?" My uncle Trystan Avila spoke first. "All nine of us are here."

I dipped my chin in acknowledgment. "Fair enough." I steepled my fingers on the large table in front of me. "It's Addison Reagan."

The three men at the table who were my brothers by blood, Cru, Snapper, and Kick, looked at me with wide eyes. "What happened?" asked the latter.

"She's been arrested," my best friend answered, saving me from revealing the emotion the words would evoke.

I swallowed and finished the sentence. "For murder."

1

Brix

Seventy-two hours earlier

The parking lot behind Stave was full, but I didn't see the one car that would've made me turn around and leave. I had no desire to see my younger sister tonight. Not that I didn't enjoy her company; Alex was fun, full of life, and smart. Sometimes too smart. Too observant. And I didn't want to be observed.

I'd much rather sneak into the wine bar, find a place to sit on the periphery of the crowded place, and watch the woman who captivated me more each time I saw her.

Addison Reagan.

She had worked for my sister long enough that she was promoted to manager. Since Alex had recently had a baby, she appreciated that Addy—as everyone but me called her—was willing to take on the new role.

No one who knew Addison well had been surprised that she was agreeable. I knew from Alex that Addison and her mom struggled financially—not that it had ever been my business.

Rather than walk in the back door used by employees, as I would've if Alex were there, I traipsed around to the front and across the bustling patio where firepits were lit to ward off the evening's chill.

I pulled my ball cap lower and kept my head down when I recognized most of those present as friends, neighbors, and business associates from the wine industry. I would still be noticed. However, my body language would communicate I wasn't interested in engaging in conversation. Something not at all unusual for me. I was known as a man of few words, especially when it came to small talk.

While I would've much preferred an out-of-the-way table indoors, the only open seat was at the bar. Coincidentally, my best friend, Noah Ridge, was on the stool beside it.

"I wondered if we'd see you tonight," said Ridge, as everyone, including me, called him.

I nodded, pulled the stool out, and took my seat. Ridge reached behind the bar, grabbed a wineglass, and poured from the unmarked open bottle in front of him. I didn't need to ask whose wine it was. One sniff, and the familiar nose of Ridge Winery's Zinfandel made my mouth salivate. I swirled the deep-red liquid, paying close attention to the edge of the dark garnet-red wine when I tilted my glass. Even in the low light, I could see the tinge of orange indicating the wine's age.

I took a sip, savoring the sweet oak, pungent red cherry, mountain bramble, and complex minerality. I closed my eyes and counted the beats of the long finish. "1991."

Ridge smiled but didn't comment. We knew one another's wine well enough that guessing vintages was easy.

"They're pouring a Cabernet flight from your winery tonight."

I picked up the tasting menu and saw the wines they'd chosen were three of my favorite Los Caballeros vintages. I couldn't help but wonder if it was Alex's idea or Addison's.

It seemed the same moment I thought about her, Addison appeared in front of me.

"Hey, Brix."

"Busy tonight."

"Always is at the end of crush."

It was the most hectic and most exhilarating time of the year in the vineyard and in the winery. The exact definition of crush varied from winemaker to winemaker. To some, it meant the entire harvest, from picking the grapes to the time the wine was bottled. To me and most of those I knew in the industry, it referred solely to when the grapes were picked and subsequently crushed.

Determining when to do that was what set winemakers apart. There was no magic to it and certainly no set schedule. When it felt right—coupled with a handful of lab tests—we picked.

Once that began, ordered chaos ensued. It sometimes meant several days in a row of round-the-clock work. Blowing off steam after the grapes were harvested was as big a part of the annual tradition as any other.

Addison eyed the glass in front of me and looked at Ridge. "By the way, help yourself to whatever you'd like behind the bar." She winked and picked up the first of three bottles containing wine I'd made.

"Which is your favorite?" I asked as she poured.

"Which is yours?" she countered as she corked one bottle before opening another.

Addison knew damn well it was a question without an answer. Like with children—not that I had any—it would be impossible to choose a favorite. There were nuances I appreciated in all three of the wines.

I watched as she pulled a wineglass caddy from the shelf, slid it around the glasses, and walked from behind the bar to deliver it. And by watched, I meant every step.

My eyes met Ridge's, and I caught his smirk when I spun my stool back around.

"You should—"

"Keep your comments to yourself," I muttered.

"All I'm saying…"

I shook my head and shot him a glare before looking in Addison's direction when she returned.

"Can I get you anything to eat?" While the question was directed at me, her gaze wasn't. Instead, she perused the crowded room.

"You're busy."

She sighed, and for the first time tonight, her eyes met mine. They were golden brown, the same color as aged tawny port when held up to the light, and framed by the rectangular red glasses I'd rarely seen her without.

"If you're hungry—"

"Hey, Addy." My sister appeared from the back and looked around the room. "Wow, you weren't kidding when you said we were packed."

"Sorry I had to call you in."

"Are you kidding? I would've been pissed if you hadn't." Alex looked from me to Ridge. "Hey, guys. What's left hangin'?" she asked while looking over the night's tasting sheet.

I rolled my eyes, and he laughed.

"We have a few vineyards of Cabernet Sauvignon, Merlot, and Sangiovese left to pick," he responded. "You're welcome to come and help tomorrow."

"Right. Because I can be in three—wait, four—places at once."

The first was at the vineyard estate she and her husband owned, Demetria. I guessed the second would be at Los Caballeros, not that Alex had helped us pick since she was in high school. The third had to be here at Stave. I had no idea what the fourth was and said so.

"Wicked Winemakers' Ball meeting tomorrow bright and early," she answered, nudging Addison. "You're in, right?"

"Um…yeah…sure."

I raised a brow at my sister when Addison left to deliver more wine.

"What?"

I shook my head.

"No, you have something to say, Gabriel, say it."

No one called me by my given name except my mother, and even that was rare. My sister was treading on thin ice with her high-handedness. Thus, I didn't respond.

Alex huffed and walked down the hallway in the direction of the kitchen. In the same way my eyes had followed Addison, Ridge's tracked my sister's every step. Also in the same way I wasn't interested in him being up in my business about the beguiling woman I couldn't keep out of my thoughts, I wouldn't serve commentary on the fact that Ridge considered my sister the one who got away.

"She's happy, right?" he mumbled.

"Do you really want me to answer that?"

Ridge shook his head and swiveled so he was facing the opposite direction, toward the patio.

I was familiar with the haunted look in his eyes and wished he'd find someone to make him forget Alex. He'd asked if she was happy, but he knew the answer.

Alex and her husband, Maddox, had been secretly dating since she was in high school. I'd been one of the few who knew about their relationship and hadn't interfered. As far as I was concerned, the feud started by our father and Maddox's should've ended years ago. In fact, had they dated openly, I doubted anyone would've cared.

It was during a short break between Mad and her that she'd gone out with Ridge, although I was well aware he'd had a crush on her for years.

"Maybe we should socialize." He motioned with his head toward the crowded patio.

"No, thanks." I finished the wine in my glass and put my hand over it when he went to pour more. "I'm headed out."

"I'll walk with you." He jammed the cork in the bottle, moved it behind the bar, and tucked a fifty under it.

Unlike when I came in, I opted to leave by the employees' entrance. As I rounded the corner, I came face-to-face with Addison.

"You're leaving?" she asked, her eyes meeting mine for the second time.

"Just stopped for a quick glass with Ridge." It was utter bullshit. There was nothing quick about me driving thirty miles each way from my family's ranch just to have a glass of wine with a man I saw almost daily. "I'm more tired than I thought I was."

She nodded in understanding. I was sure she was tired as well. While she didn't work for any of the local vineyards, her mother and stepfather owned a diner in town, where she waitressed from dawn to midafternoon before arriving at Stave and staying some nights until one in the morning. It was the reason I'd raised a brow at Alex. It was too much of her to ask for Addison's help with the annual fundraiser. I hadn't said it and wouldn't. I'd already divulged too much by my reaction alone. The last thing I wanted was my sister in my business about her employee.

"We're a pair," said Ridge, walking me to my truck. "Sunday night, and we're headed home to bed—empty beds—before eight o'clock. It's pathetic."

"You're pathetic. I'm not in the mood for Al's bullshit."

He laughed. "She can be a dog with a bone."

I opened my door. "See ya, Ridge."

"You picking tomorrow?"

"Negative. Nothing else is ready."

"Me either. Wanna ride?"

"You got it. Meet at Seahorse?" The ranch was one of the few places left with access to ride horses on the beach.

"I'll call Press in the morning."

Lavery "Press" Barrett owned Seahorse and was another friend I considered one of my best.

I waved Ridge off and was about to pull out of the parking lot when I saw Addison come out of the back door. I rolled down the window.

"Everything okay?" I asked as she studied something on her phone.

"Um, yeah. It's fine."

It was hard to tell, as dark as it was, but it looked like she might have been crying.

I pulled the truck close to the side of the building, cut the engine, and got out. As I stalked toward her, I caught her brushing a tear away.

"Anything I can help with?"

Addison shoved the phone in her back pocket and looked up at the night sky. "I just needed some air."

"Oh, yeah?" I brushed away another tear she'd missed.

"You know Dennis."

Actually, I didn't know much about her stepfather. By design. The man had moved to the Central Coast shortly before he and Addison's mother were married. Since it wasn't any of my business, I'd stopped myself from digging into the man's past. That he'd made Addison cry, though, had me wishing I had.

"What did he do?"

She let out a heavy sigh. "He and my mom fight a lot."

I took one step closer, careful not to invade her personal space. "What was the message?"

"Nothing. I need to get back inside." She rushed off before I could say anything else—even good night.

I waited near the bed of my truck for a few minutes, just to see if she'd come out if she thought I left. While I stood there, I sent a text to Ridge and Press.

What do you know about Dennis Murphy? I asked.

He's bloody Irish, Press responded. *Heard he's got the temper to go along with it. Why?* If it weren't for his English accent, always more pronounced when he was either angry or drunk, I'd likely forget that while both Press and his brother, Beau, were born in the States, they'd spent the majority of their youth and teenage years in England.

Chat tomorrow, I replied.

Copy that, he responded.

While no one in our tight group of friends had ever served in the military, other than my uncle, Trystan, who was more of a mentor to us than a peer, we'd adopted much of the lingo.

I got in my truck for the second time when my cell pinged with another message. I figured it was from Ridge, but when I looked, I saw it was from Alex.

Are you still close by?

Parking lot. Why?

Need your help. Addy needs to leave.

Be right in.

"What's going on?" I asked my sister as soon as I was inside, wishing I'd bumped into Addison first.

Alex's brow was furrowed. "An ambulance is taking her mom to the hospital. I told Sam to drive her there."

"I can take her."

"She'll be more comfortable with Samantha. Besides, they're already gone. You pour and I'll serve?"

"You got it."

"Thanks, Brix."

As much as I wanted to ask Alex what else she knew, I didn't. I'd put Ridge on it, instead.

2
Addison

I hated leaving Alex at Stave by herself, but she'd insisted my coworker and best friend, Sam, drive me to the hospital in San Luis Obispo, where our neighbor said my mom was being taken.

"Don't worry. Brix will help," she'd said, pushing me toward the door.

"I'm sorry about this," I said to Sam as we drove the half hour south.

"Seriously? Don't worry about it. You'd do the same for me." When she bit her bottom lip, I braced myself for the question. While it was easy to make up a lie about what really went on between my mom and stepfather, I knew Sam would insist on coming into the hospital with me and would likely hear the truth for herself.

She reached over and put her hand on mine. "I'm sorry, sweetie."

That she hadn't asked turned out to be harder for me to deal with. That meant she already knew.

As I'd anticipated, the moment I saw her, my mother spun a tale that she'd slipped and fallen down the stairs.

The left side of her face was badly bruised, and it looked like a cut above her swollen eye was deep enough to require stitches.

"Where's Dennis, Mom?"

"He wasn't home when it happened."

Not the question I asked, but okay. "What do you mean? I saw him at the diner this morning."

"He left shortly after you did."

"Where did he go?"

Everything about my mother's body language indicated she was lying, particularly the way her eyes wouldn't meet mine. "San Diego. He's helping his cousins remodel their kitchen."

I folded my arms. Questioning her here was pointless. I'd wait until I got her home to figure out what really happened.

A woman wearing a white coat pulled the curtain of the emergency room bay and set a laptop on the room's counter. "I'm Dr. Ambrose." She loaded an X-ray image on the screen and indicated several places on my mother's right arm. "As you can see, it's broken here, here, and here." She pointed to another bone farther up. "And it appears you broke a bone here previously."

My mother's face flushed beet red, and even when I said her name, she wouldn't look at me.

"Mrs. Murphy, I'd like to suggest you consider speaking to someone with law enforcement about your injuries," said the doctor.

"I told you, I fell down the stairs."

The doctor sighed and shook her head. "Very well, then. You'll need to wear a splint for about a week. Once the swelling goes down, we'll put a cast on. A nurse will give you your discharge instructions."

"Thank you," I murmured when my mother didn't.

"I'm sorry you had to leave work for this."

"Mom, we need to talk about Dennis."

She shook her head and shushed me. "I told you he's out of town."

While I didn't live in the house with my mother and stepfather, I heard their arguments from the apartment above the garage, where I did live. This wasn't the first time I tried to talk to her about his temper and anger issues.

"You need to file a restraining order."

My mother attempted to fold her arms and winced in pain. "Addy, please."

I rolled my eyes. "Mom, this is serious. Your arm is broken in several places. Not to mention, this isn't the first time."

She rested her head against the gurney. "Honey, please don't make me keep repeating myself."

Another woman, dressed in regular clothes, motioned me out of the bay. "I just need your mother's identification and insurance information."

I dug it out of her purse. "Be right back," I said before following the woman to the waiting room.

"How is she?" asked Sam, coming over to where I waited to get the cards back.

"Obstinate."

She scrunched her eyes. "Physically?"

"Her arm is broken in three places."

My friend studied me. "Do you think Dennis is responsible?"

"She's insisting he's out of town."

Sam raised a brow.

"I know, right? It gets worse. The doctor said it looked like she'd also broken the same arm previously."

"Yikes."

When the woman gave me back my mom's ID and insurance card, Sam motioned to a bank of chairs near us. "Come sit before you fall down."

"Do I look that bad?"

"Just tired, sweetie."

I leaned back in the chair and closed my eyes. I'd never liked Dennis. It was more than that. From the first moment I met him, I knew something was off. *Way off.* Granted, my mother attracted assholes like a magnet, starting with my father. Not that I'd ever met the man, hadn't even seen photos of him. The fact he'd left us when I was still a baby told me everything I needed to know—that he was just like the other men she seemed drawn to like the proverbial moth to a flame—a bastard.

Most came and went without making much of an impact on her life or mine. Until Dennis Murphy. Other than my father, she hadn't married any of the deadbeats until he showed up.

He was the one who'd convinced her to buy the diner. She'd had to mortgage her house to do it and hadn't asked my advice until it was a done deal.

My guess was Dennis was listed as part owner of the restaurant even though he probably didn't put a dime into it. God, why had she gotten herself mixed up with him?

The only positive thing about my mother's taste in men was that mine was the exact opposite. While she had a defective filtration system to their faults, mine was fully operational. And that meant almost no one passed muster.

One man did, but he was so far out of my league he might as well be from another planet. Not to mention, he was my boss' older brother.

Gabriel "Brix" Avila had taken my breath away from the first time I met him. He also took away my words. When he was around, I suddenly became incapable of saying anything remotely intelligent, witty, or interesting.

It wasn't just his looks, which were cover-model perfect. I was captivated by his quiet broodiness. He rarely started a conversation when he came into the wine bar—the only place other than the diner I ever saw him—and that meant if I wanted to strike one up, I had to use questions like "What can I pour you tonight?" or "Can I get you anything to eat?" I'd used that bit of brilliance tonight, in fact.

I wasn't the type of girl who would catch the attention of someone as head-turningly hot as the head winemaker and owner of Los Caballeros Vineyards.

It wasn't that I was unattractive. I just wasn't what was normally considered…attractive. I carried a few too many pounds on a too-short frame. My hair was brown. Mousy brown. Not a rich dark brown or auburn or with highlights. Just brown. I used to wear contacts, but after the long hours I worked, they'd started to irritate my eyes. I went back to wearing glasses then. Thick, ugly, red glasses that the optometrist's receptionist said looked like they belonged to someone's grandmother.

"Miss Murphy?" said a different woman from behind the front desk.

When she repeated it, I realized she might be looking for me. I stood and approached her. "I'm Peg Murphy's daughter."

"I have her discharge papers." The woman reviewed what the doctor had already said and told me a prescription for pain medication was waiting at the twenty-four-hour pharmacy attached to the hospital. The last thing she gave me was a pamphlet on domestic violence. "This isn't the first time we've seen your mom here," she said in a hushed tone of voice.

"You mean when she broke her arm?"

The woman nodded. "More than that, though."

This was news to me. I'd ask when all the other times had been, but I knew she'd already told me more than she legally should have.

The double doors opened, and my mother came out, pushed in a wheelchair by someone wearing scrubs.

"This isn't necessary. I broke my arm, not my leg," she grumbled.

"Hospital policy, ma'am."

"I'll go get the car," said Sam.

I thanked her and studied my mother while we waited. Out here, under the harsh lights of the emergency room waiting area, the bruising on her face looked so much worse. I cringed, imagining how it must've felt when Dennis hit her—because I didn't believe for a minute that she'd fallen down the stairs.

I noticed other things I hadn't before. It was obvious she hadn't given herself a manicure in weeks, but her nails still had remnants of color from the last time she did. Her hair, which she'd always colored religiously, was several weeks overdue too.

I helped her into the backseat when Sam pulled up, remembering then that I still needed to pick up her prescription.

"It's okay, Addy. I don't need it," she said when I told her and Sam I'd be right back.

"The pain might get worse, and then you'll regret not having something to take for it."

"I already have some at the house."

My eyebrows shot up. "You do?"

She looked so defeated when she rested her head against the back of the seat, my eyes filled with tears. No one should have to live with abuse—from anyone—let alone their husband. My heart broke, knowing it had been much worse than the verbal arguments I'd overheard. Dennis had actually hurt her physically to the point where she'd suffered broken bones.

The drive back to Cambria was quiet until I heard my mom snoring behind me. I looked at Sam, who looked at me, and we both had to stifle a laugh. It was terrible, given what my mom had just gone through, but with my extreme fatigue, my brain was addled.

When we parked in front of her house, I noticed two things. First, my car was also parked out front. Second, Brix's truck was too.

"What in the world?" I muttered.

"You always leave your car unlocked and your keys in it, Addy. Everyone knows that. It's a wonder no one's stolen it."

"Nobody would want it," I mumbled, trying to see whether anyone was in the other vehicle. There were no streetlights in Cambria, and the moon wasn't bright enough for me to be able to tell.

Before I could help my mother out of the backseat, the driver's door of the truck opened and Brix got out. He stalked in our direction.

"What are you doing here?"

"I brought your car."

Maybe it was that I was so damned exhausted I was punchy, but I started to laugh. "What did you do, tow it here?"

He looked at Sam and nodded in my direction. "You get her drunk on the way back?"

"I wish," said Sam. "Although—shit—I just realized it's Sunday and we have that meeting first thing in the morning."

"You aren't going."

I looked at Brix; he was talking to me. "What do you mean?"

"I told Alex you wouldn't be there."

"Ahem." Mom cleared her throat. "If you two don't mind, I really need to get some sleep."

"Of course. I'm sorry. I'll help you inside."

"Let me," said Brix.

Each of us stayed on one side of her, Brix on the side that wasn't as injured. Since it was closer, we went in through the front door rather than the back like we usually did.

"Hang on." He went ahead of us and turned on lights throughout the house. "What floor is the bedroom on?"

"This one," I told him. It made the story she'd told about falling down the stairs even less plausible, given she rarely went up to the second level.

"I've got it from here." She walked into the bedroom. "Thank you," she said to Brix and then turned to me. "I'll see you in a couple of hours, Addy."

"You aren't going to the diner tomorrow, Mom. You have a broken arm."

"We can't afford not to open, Addy."

"I'll manage."

She didn't respond, but I knew we'd be having the same argument three hours from now. She was right, though. I knew as well as she did I wouldn't be capable of managing on my own. Normally, Dennis and my mom handled the kitchen while I waited on customers. When it got busy, she helped run food to the tables. There was no way I could do all of it by myself, and we'd never be able to find help on such short notice.

"I can come in," offered Sam, whom I hadn't seen enter the house.

"Thanks, but—"

She held up her hand. "You don't have a choice, Addy. Not if you want her to stay home." She motioned with her head toward my mom's bedroom. "Just tell me what time you want me there."

"Five?" I very much doubted Sam would agree to be there that early.

"Is that what time you'll go in?" I spun in his direction at Brix's question.

"I'll be there a little earlier."

"What time?" he pressed.

I didn't want to be rude since he'd been nice enough to get my car here, but what time I went into the diner wasn't any of his business.

"Addison?"

"What?"

"I asked what time you'd be there."

Given it didn't seem he'd relent, I answered his question. "Four thirty."

"I'll see you then," he said before walking out the front door.

"Wait." I followed him. "Why?"

"You need help."

"I'll manage," I repeated the words I'd said to my mother. They didn't ring any truer now than they did then.

"Good night, Addison."

When I turned around, Sam's mouth hung open. "Is there something you want to tell me?"

"What?" I walked up the driveway to my apartment, and Sam followed.

"You and Brix?"

"There isn't a me and Brix. Alex probably made him bring my car here and…"

"Told her older brother to work at your diner?"

The idea of it was ridiculous, which is why I hadn't finished my sentence. It wasn't like Brix and I were friends. He was a customer. Sort of. I mean, he was my boss' brother, but it wasn't like he got anything for free when he came in.

We walked up the stairs on the side of the garage, and when I opened the door, Sam followed me in.

"Don't hold out on me, Addy. What's going on between you two?"

"Nothing. I swear."

Her eyebrows scrunched, and she plopped down on my sofa. *"Right."*

I looked at the time; it was one thirty, and I had to get up in less than three hours. "I need sleep."

"Me too." Sam turned and stretched out. "Grab me a pillow and a blanket."

"You don't need to stay here."

"You know it's the only way I'll get up that early."

"Sam, I appreciate this—"

"Pillow, blanket, sleep."

I got in bed after making sure my friend was settled, but doubted I'd sleep. I was as curious as she was about what Brix was up to. I could see Alex asking him to bring my car over, but nothing beyond that.

I closed my eyes, remembering every detail of how he'd looked, smelled, and felt, standing in my mother's house. While I hadn't been able to tell if he was in his truck when we pulled up, I could see every bit of his beautiful face once we went inside.

My heart beat faster, looking into his warm brown eyes and at the scruff of his beard that I knew grew fast, given how long it seemed to get between his visits to Stave. His lips, that I sneaked glances at whenever he brought a glass of wine to his mouth, made me lick my own.

His body, though—it was more perfect than his facial features. He had broad shoulders and pecs so defined they were apparent in the thin shirts he wore in the heat of the summer. Once, at a barbecue at Los Caballeros Vineyards, I'd seen his rock-hard eight-pack abs when he raised his shirt to wipe the sweat from his brow. He'd been in shorts that day, too, his powerful thighs on full display.

I couldn't stop myself from reaching between my legs, pressing against the ache always present when I pictured the way Brix had looked that day.

If only I could control my dreams and have the memory lull me to sleep.

All too soon, my alarm went off, ripping me away from the fantasy of being with Brix that my mind had been kind enough to gift me.

"No!" I heard Sam groan from the living room. "That wasn't even five minutes."

Since the diner had far better coffee than I had here, I didn't bother making a pot, relying instead on the lukewarm five-minute shower I took to wake me up. I put my uniform on and pulled my hair up in a bun. I slid my feet into my shoes at the same time Sam came out of the bathroom door.

"This will help." She pulled out her phone and turned on the playlist we'd named *Move*. It wasn't our intention, but it ended up being all Twenty One Pilots songs. We knew all the words to every one and never hesitated to sing along at the top of our lungs—as long as we were alone. One afternoon, Alex came in on a day she wasn't scheduled to and shocked us when she joined in, singing as loud as we were.

When "Trees" came up as the first song on the shuffle, we silently lip-synced and danced our way down the driveway rather than wake the neighborhood with our usual antics.

We were almost to the sidewalk when Sam came to a halt, dropped her imaginary mic, and grabbed my arm.

"What?" I gasped.

"Look," she whispered.

I followed her line of sight to where Brix leaned up against his truck that was parked directly behind my 1965 VW Bug and grinning. Brix grinning was unusual in itself. But that he was doing it before dawn and in front of my house was just weird.

"What are you doing here?" I asked when I was close enough to say it quietly.

"Waiting for you. Nice moves, by the way."

I closed my eyes and shook my head hard. I had to be dreaming. That was the only explanation. When I felt a hand on my shoulder too big to be Sam's, my lids opened slowly.

"You okay?"

"Yeah. Um, not awake yet."

I spun around when I heard the back door of my mother's house slam shut.

"Excuse me," I said to Brix before stalking over to my mother, who was walking down the driveway in our direction. "You need to stay home, Mom. If you don't, the swelling won't go down in your arm and they won't be able to put a cast on it."

She looked beyond me to Sam and Brix and then up and down the street. "I need to go to the diner." Her eyes were wide and her voice strained.

I put my hand on her shoulder like Brix had done to me. "Mom? What's going on?"

"I can't just sit here and do nothing. I need to be at the diner. Please, Addy." Her eyes, full of tears, continued to dart around the neighborhood.

"Of course, Mom." Once again, Brix helped me get her to Sam's car, which was easier for her to get in and out of than my bug. "Have you heard from Dennis?"

Her eyes met mine. "No. Why?"

"Just wondering."

"We need to go, or we won't open on time."

"Okay, but you have to promise you won't do anything to exacerbate your injury."

She didn't promise. In fact, she didn't make another sound until we walked into the kitchen and turned the lights on. Even then, she didn't speak; she only let out a breath I hadn't realized she was holding.

3
Brix

Peg Murphy was terrified. It was easy enough to tell by her demeanor. She moved as though she expected someone to jump from the shadows and grab her.

Given my gut told me the woman's husband could show up at any moment, I proceeded with caution more than fear.

That was only one of the reasons I was here, one of the reasons I'd stayed parked on Addison's street long after she and Sam had gone inside. It wasn't until Ridge showed up to keep watch that I went home long enough to shower and change. I was tense the entire hour and a half I was gone. Like Peg had, I exhaled in relief when I returned to Cambria and Ridge reported all was quiet.

The call I'd received last night from Press was what made me go directly to Addison's neighborhood after I helped Alex close up Stave.

"Dennis Murphy is up to his neck in it," he'd said.

"Meaning?"

"Big-time gambling debts, some of which go back to the time before he married Addison's mom. As you've probably already guessed, Dennis Murphy is an alias."

"What's his real name?"

"I'm sorry to say that remains a mystery."

"Okay. Back to the money. How much are we talking?"

"Close to two hundred grand, which would explain the million-dollar life insurance policy he took out in his wife's name a couple of weeks ago."

"Who's the beneficiary?"

"Patrick Sullivan."

"Lemme guess. Same DOB as Murphy."

"One of several aliases, it seems. Working to confirm it now, along with what name *does* appear on his birth certificate. Rap sheet a mile long under Murphy *and* Sullivan, by the way. Mostly petty stuff, which is why he's slipped through the cracks."

I wondered if Peg's husband had intended her injuries to be far worse. Maybe—*probably*—he'd pushed her down the stairs.

"What do you want to do, Brix?" Press asked.

"Keep watch," I'd told him, and that's exactly what I'd continue to do. "See if you can get a twenty on him."

"Roger that."

While Addison got her mother settled in a chair from which she could oversee the kitchen, I asked Sam how I could be the most help.

"Do you know how to cook?" she asked.

I raised a brow.

"What?" Her eyes widened.

"What do you think wine making is?"

"Not cooking."

"Well, you're wrong. I go out to the 'garden' and pick the ripest fruit, bring it into my 'kitchen,' and whip up something people pay a great deal of money to sample."

"Yeah, okay, Chef Brix, but do you know how to cook *food*?"

"With eight mouths to feed and a husband out in the vineyard before sunrise and after sunset, as the oldest, Gabe had to learn so he could help me," I heard my mother say as she swept in through the back door. "Good morning, dear." She patted my cheek.

"Mrs. Avila?" gasped Addison before glaring at me.

I held up my hands. "Tell her, Mama, I had nothing to do with you being here."

My mother made a beeline for Peg instead. "My daughter, Alex, told me you had an accident. ¡Oh, Dios!" she cried when she stood in front of her. My mom, bless her heart, recovered quickly from her shock. "Did you know that back when George first opened this place, I used to work for him? In fact, most of the recipes are mine."

Since my sister had suggested she show up here, I hoped my mother would stop talking long enough to actually help.

"Are the recipes really hers?" Sam asked.

I laughed. "It's doubtful."

She shook her head and walked over to join the conversation between Addison's mother and mine, leaving me alone to talk to the woman who was studying me.

"Do you have something to say?" I asked, walking closer.

"Who are you?"

Since she spoke barely above a whisper, I took another step. "What do you mean?"

"No offense, Brix—I mean that sincerely—but… why are you here?"

"When you asked me a similar question before, I told you I'm here because you need help."

She busied herself turning on ovens and some of the other equipment.

I followed. "Does my being here bother you?"

"It isn't that."

"What is it?"

"You're acting so…different."

I smiled. "In what way?"

Addison stopped what she was doing and put her hands on her hips. "In *that* way. You just smiled. I don't know how many times I've waited on you, and I don't think I've seen you smile once."

I was about to argue and say she was wrong, but she probably wasn't. I didn't smile very often, which I suppose was one of the reasons it felt so good to be doing it now. I was usually so caught up in my work at the winery. I was often too preoccupied to pay attention to things that might have made me laugh. Since I was here to help Addison, I didn't feel the same kind of pressure. This was something I wanted to do—it wasn't my livelihood or that of my family.

"I smile."

She rolled her eyes and looked over to where our mothers and Sam were chatting. "I better get busy."

"Put me where you want me."

When Addison flushed, it told me everything I needed to know. She'd picked up on my double entendre, recognized I was flirting with her, and she liked it.

She'd always done a great job of acting completely professional around me. She rarely made conversation, and if she did, it was typically to ask what I wanted to eat or drink. When she'd teased Ridge about helping himself to whatever he wanted behind the bar, I had to admit I felt a twinge of jealousy. It was the most I'd ever seen her flirt with someone, especially when she added the wink. As much as I wanted Ridge to find someone who made him forget my sister, I'd never considered it might be Addison. *My* Addison.

My mother clapped her hands, jarring me. "Why are you standing around, doing nothing? We need to get busy, *mijo*."

I followed her over to the sink and washed my hands. "What am I doing?"

"You can start the dough." She pointed to an industrial-size mixer as if that was enough information for me to get at it.

"I'll help," said Addison, motioning to the walk-in cooler. "Everything is ready to go. We just need to put it in the ovens."

"Let me get that," I said when she pulled out an oversized and heavily laden baking sheet.

"There are eleven more." She walked out, and I followed with one of the remaining sheets. "They slide into the racks, and then we put the whole thing in the walk-in oven."

"Wouldn't it be easier to take the rack into the cooler and load them there?"

Addison glared at me, grabbed the rack, and pulled it behind her. I heard her mimicking me but in a singsong voice. "Wouldn't it be easier to take it in there?"

When I laughed out loud, she reacted as if I'd frightened her. "What?" I said, looking behind me.

"First smiling, now laughing?"

"I laugh," I said in the same way I told her I smiled earlier—with an utter lack of conviction. She responded with yet another eye roll.

"You do that a lot," I said when she wheeled the now-full cart out.

"What?"

"Roll your eyes at me."

She shrugged. "It isn't just you."

"Let me get that," I said when she approached the ovens. She punched a code into a keypad and opened the door for me.

When I came out a few seconds later, I didn't see her. I closed the door behind me and studied the pad. It appeared the temperature had already been set, so I pressed the start button.

"I think we have this under control if you want to take off." She motioned to our mothers and Sam, who were prepping vegetables.

"I'll stick around in case it gets busy."

She looked as if she was going to say something else, but appeared to change her mind. Instead, she walked toward the back door and motioned for me to follow her outside.

"Can I ask you something?"

"Of course."

"Does my mother seem agitated to you?"

That she'd asked me rather than Sam made my chest swell. "Very."

"I thought so too. Last night, I told you she and Dennis fight a lot…"

"I remember."

"It's worse than that. I didn't realize how much worse until we were at the hospital." She folded her arms and looked out at the ocean across the road. "The nurse gave me this." When she pulled a folded piece of paper out of her back pocket and handed it to me, I saw it was a domestic violence pamphlet. "She said my mom had been there before for treatment. More than once."

"You had no idea?"

She sighed and her brow furrowed. "It was probably on the nights I was working at Stave. Although I think I would've noticed if she'd broken her arm." Addison's eyes filled with tears.

I wanted to reach out, pull her into my arms, and tell her she wasn't alone. That I was here because I was worried about both her mother and her, but our relationship wasn't at the point where I thought she'd feel comfortable if I tried to embrace her.

I still hadn't decided whether to tell her about the insurance policy her stepfather took out on her mother or about his gambling debts. I also hadn't heard if either Ridge or Press got a lead on his real name or where the man was.

"I'm afraid to leave her alone." She attempted to blink her tears away. "I'm probably overreacting."

"I don't think you are."

"Alex doesn't think so either, does she? That's why she asked you to come to the house last night and why you're here now."

"Well…"

"I knew it," she muttered.

While it would've been easier to let her believe her logical assumption, I didn't want to. I wanted Addison to know I'd made the decision on my own. "Alex had nothing to do with last night or this morning."

Her eyes opened wide. "I don't understand."

"I'm here because I want to be. Because I want to help you. Not because my sister asked me to."

"What about your mom?"

I chuckled. "Now, that *was* Alex's doing."

Her eyes bored into mine. "You're different than I thought."

"How so?" I braced myself for what I innately knew would make me feel like an asshole.

"You're nice."

I could tell she regretted saying it as soon as she had.

"I'm sorry if I hurt your feelings."

I shook my head. "I deserved to hear it."

"I could've softened the blow a little and said you're *nicer*."

I laughed, which she appeared to be getting more used to, although it still seemed to surprise her.

Had I really laughed that little when I was around her? It certainly wasn't intentional. The weight of my responsibilities just dragged me down more often than not.

"How many brothers do you have?" she blurted.

Her question surprised me. Did she think one of them was nicer than I was? "I'm trying to figure out the segue."

"I just wondered."

"Five brothers, one sister."

"Which ones do you have breakfast here with occasionally?"

"Snapper and Kick more than anyone else. When they're in town."

"Do they travel a lot?"

"A couple of years ago, they partnered in vineyard property and are dabbling in wine making, so they're here more than they were. They're still team ropers on the circuit, though."

She looked confused.

"Rodeo."

"Oh." She nodded slowly. "Um, we should go back in."

"Before we do, I want you to know that until your stepfather resurfaces, and even after that, I'll be keeping an eye out."

"Okay," she whispered.

"No more asking why I'm here or saying it's okay for me to leave?"

Her cheeks paled rather than flushed. "Do you plan to keep that close of an eye?"

I took a step toward her. "I do."

"Okay," she whispered a second time before going inside with me on her heels.

4

Addison

When we walked into the kitchen, Mrs. Avila called Brix over to talk to her while I went back to my prep work. Every so often, I'd glance in their direction, but Brix's back was to me. I could tell by the look on his mother's face their conversation was serious.

Outside, in the bright light of the sun, I saw the gray creeping into Brix's dark-brown hair. It made me wonder how old he was. I knew Alex was thirty-three and she had two other brothers between Brix and her. Was he forty? It sounded so old to me until I thought about how soon I'd turn thirty. Was ten years too much of an age difference for people to date?

I shook my head and laughed at myself. As if Brix would ever want to date me.

"What's funny?" Sam asked.

"Me. I'm an idiot."

Her brow furrowed.

"It's nothing. I swear."

She motioned toward Brix. "It's nice of him to be here."

"It's nice of you to be here too."

"I'm your best friend, Addy. As if I wouldn't help." She rolled her eyes.

"He said I roll my eyes at him a lot."

"You do."

"You just did it to me."

"We both do it. Mighty passive-aggressive of us, don't ya think?" She pulled off a still-warm piece of one of the muffins, popped it in her mouth, and nudged me with her shoulder. "You have to let people help you, Addy. You and your mom can't do this alone."

I got it, but it still felt wrong to allow Brix not only to help but also to look out for my mom and me. I just couldn't bring myself to say so more than I already had. Especially after he'd agreed she seemed agitated.

I knew the reason her eyes had been darting up and down the street before we left home earlier was because she was looking for Dennis, worried he was lurking nearby.

Given how much the idea frightened me, I could only imagine it terrified her. I wished she would be honest with me about the abuse. Maybe then we could get the right kind of help. Even a restraining order against him. But I knew she wouldn't. I'd read up on why women stay in abusive relationships, and that was when I'd believed it was only verbal, not physical. I could see the signs clearly with my own mother.

Low self-esteem, definitely. I also recalled that after their fights, he would be extra sweet to her for several days. Way more than usual.

There were so many other things I recognized. Possibly, she felt pressure to stay in the relationship rather than go back to being single. Or maybe she thought things would eventually get better. Or—worse—she was too afraid to kick him out.

I looked up from where I was about to review the menu and make mental notes of what still needed to be prepped, and found her studying me. When our eyes met, she looked away.

Why? Was she embarrassed? Ashamed? Or was she feeling resentful of me for interfering?

I was never given a choice about working at the diner. When it reopened under Dennis and my mom's ownership, she *told* me rather than asked that she expected me to waitress. I was twenty-six at the time and certainly capable of saying no. I never would have, though. I knew they needed my help.

I got to keep my tips, which meant I usually made at least minimum wage, but I'd never make enough, working here, that I could quit my job at Stave. I wouldn't want to anyway. I loved being there, even if half the time, I was exhausted from the number of fifteen-hour days in a row I came in.

"So, why did you and Brix go outside a few minutes ago?"

I sighed. "I asked him if he thought my mother seemed agitated."

"Ya think?" she whispered, looking over at her like I had. "She's a nervous wreck. When you came back in, she looked like a deer in headlights until she saw it was the two of you. I wonder what really happened last night."

I did too. I also wondered how my mom would react when Dennis reappeared.

As the day went on, I tried not to feel guilty about Brix being at the diner, but I couldn't help it. This was the busiest time of the year at any winery, and instead of taking care of his business, he was helping with ours.

I didn't know what to do about it, though. I'd already told him he could leave, that we had it handled, but he'd refused. He'd also basically asked me not to say it again.

The biggest problem I saw, moving forward, was that Mrs. Avila, Sam, and Brix couldn't continue helping us. Later, after we closed, I'd ask my mother when Dennis was supposed to be home. Not that I believed he was really in San Diego. Well, he might be, but not for the reason she'd said.

Regardless of why he left, it made no sense. He knew she and I wouldn't be able to manage running the diner without him.

The only thing remotely logical was that he took off because he knew he'd gone too far with whatever happened between them and was afraid he would get in trouble.

Whatever the answers were about Dennis, it didn't change the fact that in order to stay open, we'd have to hire a cook. My mother certainly wouldn't be able to do it with a broken arm. But where would we find someone who could start right away?

I looked around the kitchen, stunned that everything was ready for us to open. We still had thirty minutes before that happened.

I sat on a stool, rested my elbow on the counter, and put my head in my hand. Once the regular crowd began shuffling in, I wouldn't have time to think about our dilemma; I'd be too busy. Not that I was getting anywhere, thinking about it now.

My head spun around when I heard the back door creak open, relieved as well as surprised when Alex walked in, carrying Coco.

"She's getting so big," cried Sam, rushing over to see the three-month-old.

"And heavy," said Alex, handing the baby to my best friend when she put her arms out. "How's it going?" she walked closer and asked.

"Okay. Thanks for asking your mom to come this morning and for sending Brix over last night."

"Brix came over last night?" She seemed genuinely surprised. "When?"

"He was there when we got back from the hospital. He brought my car."

"Hmm. Interesting."

"You didn't ask him to?"

"No, and now I feel like shit that I didn't." She looked over at him and their mother. "I should go say good morning. We'll talk more in a minute." She looked around until her gaze rested on my mom. "Oh, it's worse than I thought," she whispered.

"I know." I really didn't know what else to say. It *was* worse. It was awful.

"On a positive note, it looks like you're set to open."

"We are, thanks to Sam, your mom, and Brix."

"Maybe we could have a quick meeting."

"Alex," Brix growled, overhearing her. "You're going to have to face the fact that Addison won't be able to help with the fundraiser this year."

Her back had been to me, but she turned around. "Wow," she mouthed with a smile and a wink before turning back to her brother. "Is that so? I didn't realize you spoke for Addy."

Brix looked from her to me and back again. "I don't speak for her. I just pointed out she doesn't have time."

"Like I said," she responded, shaking her head before leaning down to kiss her mother's temple. "Good morning, Mama. Thanks for being here."

Mrs. Avila patted my mother's leg. "Peg and I have been talking and have some ideas about how to keep the diner open while her arm heals."

"You do?" I blurted.

"Well, it wasn't just your mom and me. Gabriel too."

His eyes met mine, but I had no idea what he might be thinking.

"I'm still not sure about this, Lucia," said my mother.

"Give me a few more minutes, and I'll convince you."

"What's going on?" I asked Brix when he walked over to me.

"A couple things." He motioned for me to follow him out the kitchen door.

Once I had, I stood with my arms folded.

"Until your mom is back on her feet, so to speak, my mom is going to help in the kitchen."

I opened my mouth to argue with him, but closed it when he raised his hand.

"She loves this place, and I think she was heartbroken when George said he didn't need her help anymore. After talking to her more about it, I do think at least some of the recipes really were hers."

"I don't know the state of the diner's finances or how much my mom will be able to afford to pay her."

"I know, Addison. She does too. This is about friends helping friends."

"I don't think your mom and mine are friends." The two definitely ran in different social circles.

"You're wrong. And it isn't just our moms. Alex is your friend." He leaned closer. "I would be too if you'd let me."

"What about when Dennis comes back?"

He looked out at the ocean. "I don't know. That's complicated."

I agreed; it was complicated, but it seemed like he knew something I didn't. I wouldn't ask now, though. I needed to get back inside and turn on the open sign.

5

Brix

When Addison left, I walked across the road and sat on a bench overlooking Moonstone Beach. I was overstepping. That was obvious even to me, but I couldn't help myself. For as long as I'd known her—not that I could recall when we'd first met—Addison had worked her ass off. There were times when I walked into Stave, saw how exhausted she looked, and wanted to tell her I'd handle the tasting bar so she could go home and rest. I never did, though, as much because it wasn't my place as it was because I knew she'd refuse.

On the other hand, the owners of the vineyards on the Central Coast helped each other all the time, without expecting any kind of compensation or payback.

When another owner needed extra hands to pick, we'd send whatever crew we could, myself included. When some of the wineries lost their vineyards in a wildfire, the rest of us pitched in and gave them juice so they could still bottle and release wine that year. If equipment was down, someone would lend theirs. It was just what we did.

Helping Addison and her mom was no different. They'd just have to learn to accept that when it came to bringing in the harvest, getting wine in bottles, or keeping the diner open, the community would come together to make it happen.

It wouldn't be just my family. My cousins, who owned vineyard property next to our ranch, would pitch in. Their mother was my mom's twin, and they'd been raised the same way my siblings and I were. When help was needed, we gave it.

The same with the Butlers, whose property bordered ours on the other side. Once Laird and Sorcha Butler heard Addison and her mother needed help, nothing would keep Sorcha from showing up just like my mom had. I laughed, thinking about the two of them—plus Aunt Esmeralda—showing up on the same day. Talk about too many cooks in the kitchen.

Later, once we'd gotten through breakfast and lunch, I'd sit down with Peg, Addison, my mom, and whoever else showed up between now and then, and explain what our plans were.

The one thing I wouldn't be prepared to talk about, however, was what would happen when her stepfather showed up.

There wasn't much for me to do once the doors were opened to customers, so I sat at the counter, poured a cup of coffee, and grabbed one of the olallieberry muffins the place was famous for. In fact, that was its name—the Olallieberry Diner and Bakery.

"How's everything going?" Ridge asked when he came in and took a seat beside me.

"Pretty good, I think." I turned to face him and lowered my voice. "Any update on Murphy?"

"We think we have a lead on where he is."

"Where?"

"Mojave."

There wasn't a hell of a lot out in the city with the same name as the desert, other than a graveyard for old airplanes and a shit ton of criminals. I'd once heard a statistic that the city was in the sixth percentile for safety—meaning ninety-four percent of all cities in the United States were safer than Mojave was. It made sense he went there, for that reason alone.

"Where'd the lead come from?"

"Through Snapper and Kick. Evidently, they both sent out messages with his photo."

That made sense too. My youngest brothers were highly ranked PRCA—Professional Rodeo Cowboys Association—team ropers. The network of those they knew from competing was vast and from all walks of life.

"One guy said Murphy has family out there."

Another thing that wasn't a surprise. Lowlife asshole that he was.

"Someone else said they were pretty sure they saw him coming out of a convenience store this morning. At least, the guy looked a lot like him."

"Does Press have time to stay on this?"

Ridge nodded. "Beau's in town, so he's on it too."

Press' younger brother lived in Napa Valley, where he managed the Barrett family's northern-based wine operations. He came down to visit Press' Seahorse Ranch as often as he could, though.

"What can I do to help with the diner?" Ridge asked.

"Can you be back here at two when they close?"

"Don't see why not."

"We'll talk about it then."

"Hey, Ridge," said Addison, coming over and setting a coffee cup in front of him that she filled before grabbing the four creams he typically asked for.

"Hey, Addy."

"Can I get you the usual?"

"Yes, please."

"What the fuck?" I mumbled when she walked away. "How the hell does Addison know how you take your coffee and your 'usual' breakfast order?"

"Don't you realize how often I meet you here? You'd think it was the only place in town that served food in the morning."

"But your *usual* breakfast order?"

"Shit, Brix, I always order the exact same thing. Is your head really that far up your ass that you've never noticed?"

Not once. What other people ate wasn't something I paid any attention to. Why would I? "I guess if I want something to eat, I'll have to get it myself."

Ridge chuckled and shook his head. "Sometimes you are the least aware person I know."

"What do you mean?"

"How much coffee have you had?"

"One cup." At least since I sat down. I lost count of how many I'd had between five and seven.

"Addy knows better than to ask what you want until you've had at least two and finished your muffin that I bet she set in front of you, warm from the oven."

"Sam did."

"Did you ask her for it?" He studied me for a second. "You didn't. Which means Addy told her."

"That's bullshit."

"Oh, yeah? Watch and listen. Hey, Addy, got a sec?"

"Of course," she said, setting a glass of orange juice he hadn't ordered in front of Ridge and pouring me another cup of coffee.

"What does Brix usually order for breakfast?"

She looked at me, and her eyes scrunched. "It varies. Why?"

"Hang on. Are you going to ask if he wants to order?"

She scowled at him. "In a minute. Why?"

"Why not now?"

Addison set the pot of coffee on the counter hard enough that some splashed out of it. "What are you up to, Ridge?"

"Proving a point. Come on, just answer. Why not now?"

"Because he doesn't like to order right away," she answered through gritted teeth.

"When does he?"

I put my hand on my friend's arm. "Point proven. You can stop now."

Addison picked up the pot and stomped away.

"You made her mad."

He laughed. "Her being mad at *me* doesn't bother you a bit."

"You got that right."

By the time two o'clock rolled around, not only had Aunt Esmeralda shown up, Sorcha Butler was here as was her oldest daughter, Skye. That wasn't all, though. More cars were pulling in.

"What's going on?" Addison asked. "We're closed."

"Town meeting," said Ridge, who'd been back about five minutes.

"Come with me," I said when she glared at him. We went out the back door for the third time today. "Word has gotten out that you and your mom need some help."

"But—"

I put my finger on her lips, trying not to lose my train of thought when I felt their softness for the first time. "It's what we do, Addison. What we've always done."

"We're not vineyard owners."

"That makes no difference. You're part of the community."

When she looked away, my fingers itched to touch her again, turn her head back toward me.

"I don't know what to say. This is all so surreal." She looked into my eyes. "Thank you, Brix."

I watched her walk away, wishing I had been smart enough—brave enough—to answer her the way I wanted to. With a kiss.

6
Addison

"Got a minute?" asked Alex, who had come back as well. I wondered if she had the baby with her this time. I hadn't gotten the chance to hold Coco earlier.

"Of course."

Alex looked out the window by the back door. "He's gone around the front. Good," I heard her mutter. She turned to me, put her hands on my shoulders, and looked me in the eye.

"You're worrying me," I said when she didn't speak right away.

"Listen, I know as well as anyone that you don't have time to help with the Wicked Winemakers' Ball this year. To be honest, almost everything is ready for the big event. And it won't be a problem to get someone to cover for you that night. God, I can't believe it's less than two weeks away. Anyway, there's just one very small thing I want you to do. By the looks of it, you might have it wrapped up later today."

I sighed. "Alex, what are you talking about?"

"Brix. I want you to talk him into being in the bachelor auction."

"What?"

"You heard me. Talk Brix into participating this year. I bet he'd pull in ten grand easy."

"Alex! No!"

"Come on, Addy. The guy worships the ground you walk on. If you're the one who asks, I have no doubt he'll agree."

"How many times have you asked in the past and he's turned you down?"

"That's different. He barely tolerates me."

"No."

Alex took her hands off my shoulders and clasped them in front of her. "*Please.* I'm begging. Just ask him. I'll take care of everything else. I'm telling you, he'll probably break the record for the highest bid. Think of what that money will mean for the Children's Hospital. How can you say no?"

This was why Alex chaired the annual fundraiser. No one could say no to her. Except her oldest brother. He'd turned her down every year since she took over the event.

While the silent auction and other live auction items—like travel packages to exotic locations or hot-air balloon rides followed by a private dinner at a winery—brought in a decent amount of money, it was the bachelor auction that pulled in the big cash. The dates the guys dreamed up were pretty spectacular too, but that wasn't important to the kind of women who typically bid on them.

Even without Brix, Alex had an impressive lineup of guys she convinced to sign up year after year. As much as some of last year's bidders may have hoped otherwise, I hadn't heard of a single participant who'd been "taken off the market" since the last ball.

Three of Brix's younger brothers—Enzo, Salazar, and Rascon—were participants, along with four of the hottest winemakers I'd ever met—Noah Ridge, Vaile Oliver, Lavery Barrett, and his brother, Beau. I'd heard a few years ago a couple of the Butler boys participated, but they were all married now. I'd also heard that every one of the bachelors were millionaires. Actually, the rumor was they were all billionaires, but I had no idea how much truth there was to it.

Alex was usually able to sprinkle in enough of the area's other winemakers to make it an even ten, but

Brix had never been one of them. Neither had two of their other brothers, Cristobal and Trevino. Cris, I knew, was a doctor and lived in Palo Alto. I had no idea if he was single or married. I wasn't sure why Trevino didn't agree to do it. Maybe Alex hadn't asked him since he wasn't an actual winemaker. From what I understood, he ran the Los Cab tasting room.

"Should I assume your silence means you're thinking of the best way to ask him?"

I laughed and shook my head. "It means I'm trying to figure out how to get you to take no for an answer."

"Just as long as you don't take no for an answer from Brix, I'll be happy."

I rolled my eyes, making a note that I had done so. "Sorry," I muttered.

"What for?"

"Brix pointed out how often I do that."

"Do what?"

"Roll my eyes at people."

Alex studied me and shook her head slowly. "Oh, sister. He isn't the only one who's got it bad."

"What are you talking about?"

"You and Brix. I'm going to love watching this play out. It didn't occur to me before how perfect you are for each other. I don't know why it didn't. It's so obvious."

I laughed. "If you think blowing this kind of smoke up my skirt is going to convince me to ask him, you're crazy."

"Ask who what?" The man himself approached.

"Addy? Do you have a question for my brother?"

"Nope, I sure don't." I left the two of them together and went straight into the walk-in cooler. I needed a minute alone to simmer down.

While I'd never call her out on it more directly than I had, the bullshit Alex was spewing about how Brix and I were perfect for each other pissed me off. Did she really think I was that much of an idiot that I'd buy into what she was trying to manipulate me into doing? There was no way in hell I'd ask Brix to be in the auction. Given how many times he'd turned his own sister down, it was obvious it wasn't something he wanted to do.

"Addison? Are you okay?" When Brix walked into the cooler, I pretended to be counting the sheets of pastries we had left to bake tomorrow. It was something

I had to do anyway; I just hadn't thought of it until that moment.

"I'm good. How are you? You must be exhausted. You can take off, you know. I mean, we're closed." I vomited all those words and managed not to look at him. Bravo, Addy.

"Hey." He stepped closer. Too close. "What was that between you and Alex?"

"Nothing."

"Had to have been something for you to hide out in a giant freezer."

"I'm not hiding out. I'm doing inventory."

"Yeah? You could've counted everything in here ten times by now. Come on, you're *freezing*."

Brix took my hand, and it felt so warm. Hot actually. Scorchingly hot. The heat spread throughout my body. He didn't let go, even after we were outside, at what was becoming our meeting place.

"Tell me what Alex said to you."

I tried to pull my hand away, but he wouldn't let go. In fact, he grabbed the other one and stepped so close our bodies were almost touching.

"Tell me what Alex did to upset you."

"She didn't upset me."

"Yes, she did. Now tell me why."

"It isn't worth talking about. She asked me to do something, and I said I couldn't."

"Something to do with me."

He didn't say it as a question, so I didn't feel the need to respond.

"What?"

I tried again to shake my hands free, but he held tight.

"There are a whole lot of people inside, waiting to talk to both of us, but I have no intention of letting you go until you tell me what Alex asked you to do."

"It isn't that big of a deal," I said, this time jerking my hands from his. "She wanted me to ask you to be in the Wicked Winemakers' Bachelor Auction, and I told her I wouldn't."

He smirked. "Why not?"

My eyes opened wide, and I put my hands on my hips. "Are you serious right now? *Why not?* Because she's asked you a million times, and you've always refused. She was trying to manipulate me into asking, and I didn't want any part of it."

I looked out of the corner of my eye and saw more people walking into the diner; they'd obviously heard my outburst.

"Great." I shook my head and looked at the ground. "Now everyone will think I'm a crazy person."

"Yes."

"Right! Batshit crazy."

"No. I mean, yes, I'll be in the auction. However, I have a few stipulations."

I stared at him, mouth hanging open. I snapped it closed and spun around so my back was to him. "You know who really is batshit crazy? You and Alex. You two can sort this crap out on your own."

I was headed inside when I heard him speak again.

"One stipulation involves you, Addison."

I wanted to pull my hair out, crawl into a hole, and never come out. "No. Whatever it is, the answer is no."

"We'll talk about it later," he said as he joined me at the door. "Come on, let's go." He grabbed my hand and pulled me with him.

"You're infuriating," I mumbled.

What did he do? He *laughed.*

7
Brix

While Addison seemed stunned by the number of people who showed up at the diner to help in whatever way they could, I wasn't surprised. This community was always ready to lend a hand as soon as they heard one was needed.

Addison had no idea how many lives she'd touched while working at Stave, especially since she was promoted to manager and it became her decision which wineries to feature each night. She took the time to taste each wine she served, form her own opinions, and then if a customer had a question, she was prepared to answer.

As much as I'd wished I could get her attention long enough to have more than a superficial conversation, I understood that when I came in to either Stave or the diner, she was working and didn't have time—or the interest—to socialize.

The bachelor auction was going to change all that, though. I intended to take full advantage of her asking, even though I'd forced her to. Regardless, I had a plan, and by the time this meeting was over, I'd put it into action.

I didn't, though. Addison and her mom were inundated by people wanting to personally offer their support. As tired as I was beginning to feel, I was sure the two women were even more exhausted. Instead of pressing my cause, once everyone left, I offered to escort them home.

I could tell Addison's first inclination was to say it wasn't necessary. However, the fear I was sure she'd also noticed in her mom's eyes kept her from doing so.

"We've got tonight covered," said Ridge, walking up to my truck as I was getting ready to leave.

"As much as I'd like to say I'll handle it, I know better."

"You're dead on your feet, my friend."

I couldn't remember the last time I'd slept. Between the wine crush and spending the previous night camped out in front of Addison's mother's house, the days were a blur. "I appreciate this, man."

"Thank your brothers. Snapper and Kick volunteered before anyone even asked."

"Tag-teaming is a good idea. Addison lives in the apartment above the garage."

"You don't say."

My eyes met Ridge's, and before I could light into him, he grinned. "Go home and sleep, Brix. Before you're too exhausted to drive."

"I need to talk to her first."

"Do you want me to wave her over?"

I shook my head. "Peg is in the car with her. I'll head to the house, let Addison know what's going on, then head home. By the way, make sure Snapper and Kick take another thorough look of the main house and Addison's apartment before we get there."

"Roger that."

I wasn't a block from the diner when my cell rang with a call from Alex. "What?" I barked when I hit the call-accept button on my dash.

"Hey, that isn't very nice."

"Come on, Al. I don't know when I last slept or even if I'll be able to once I'm back at Los Cab."

"That's why I'm calling. Maddox is on his way, and Naughton is already there."

Maddox Butler was Alex's husband and Naughton his younger brother. The two were renowned not just in this valley but around the world for their combined knowledge in both viticulture and wine making.

"What's Naughton saying?"

"He told Mad he thinks we should pick vineyards forty, forty-one, and forty-three."

"Give the crew the go-ahead and let them know I'll be there as soon as I can."

"No, Gabriel. You need to go home and sleep. Mad is bringing teams from both Demetria and Butler Ranch. They'll be done before sunup."

When my father died, it was Maddox Butler who'd stepped up and helped us finish the harvest that year. He'd worked by my side through the entire crush. I trusted him and his brother more than anyone else in the valley. If Naughton said it was time to pick, I had no doubt it was.

"Where's Enzo?" My middle brother was our second-label winemaker and also handled sales for Los Cab.

"I know I should let you leave."

I shook my head.

"I'd just feel better if you stayed." Addison took a deep breath and let it out slowly. "Do you know how hard that was for me to say?"

"I do." I stepped around the sofa and stood in front of her. "Get some sleep. I'll be right here if you need me. My brothers will make sure no one gets anywhere near the house."

"Thank you, Brix."

"You're welcome, Addison."

She was almost to the hallway when she turned around. "I'm sorry I said you weren't nice." She shook her head. "That isn't what I said, but you know what I mean, and I'm sorry."

"Apology accepted."

"There are pillows and blankets in the chest by the window."

"Thanks. Good night…" It was on the tip of my tongue to say "sweetheart," but I stopped myself. I watched her walk down the hallway and into the bedroom I wished I was sharing with her.

I wasn't sure how long I'd been asleep when my phone rang with a call from Ridge.

"Yeah?" I said, sitting up on the sofa.

"Brix, the diner is on fire. Where are you?"

"I'm at Addison's." I stood and went out onto the landing, hoping I didn't wake her. "Where are you?"

"On the scene. It's bad."

"Have you talked to either of my brothers?"

"Not yet. I'll call Snapper next. Oh and, Brix, keep Addy there. There's nothing she can do. It's a total loss."

"Shit." I ended the call with Ridge when I saw my youngest brother was calling. "Hey, Kick. I just got off the phone with Ridge."

"So you know the diner's on fire."

"Affirmative."

"What do you want us to do?"

"Stay put, and I'll do the same."

"What about Peg?"

I looked down at the dark house, praying she was fast asleep. "Have you seen or heard anything?"

"Negative. Both Snapper and I have been surveilling the property for the last eight hours. No one has been in or out."

"Keep me posted," I said, ending the call when I heard movement from inside the apartment.

"Brix?"

I went in and closed the door behind me. "Yeah, baby?"

I tried to keep my eyes focused on her face when she came out in a barely there tank top and a skimpy pair of boy shorts. I knew by the look in her eyes and the way she dropped her hand with her cell in it that she knew what happened.

"Sam called and said she heard the diner is on fire."

"I just got the same call from Ridge. He said it's pretty far gone."

"What?"

"I'm so sorry, Addison," I said, stepping closer to her.

"I need to tell my mom."

I agreed but wished I'd asked Kick to do it while I had him on the phone. I wanted to confirm her mom was safe and sound before I let Addison go into the house.

She was headed toward the door when she must've realized what she was wearing. "I need to grab some clothes."

After she went to change, I sent Kick a text.

Any sign of Peg?

Yep. Snapper is talking to her now.

I sighed with relief.

"Grab your shoes, baby," I said when I saw her headed outside barefoot but thankfully in a sweatshirt and jeans. It was the second time I'd used the term of endearment, and she either hadn't noticed or it wasn't registering with everything she had on her mind.

"Do you know what happened?" she asked, sliding her feet into a pair of moccasins that sat by the door.

"I don't. Ridge is on the scene, though. We can call him after we talk to your mom."

"Okay."

"Let me go ahead of you. The stairs will be slick." I held the rail and took my time going down the wooden steps, wet from the moisture of the nearby ocean. They needed to be repainted and anti-slip treads added.

When we got to the bottom, Peg was headed in our direction.

"Addy!" she cried. "It's gone. Everything. *We've lost everything!"*

I nodded when Addison's stunned eyes met mine before she embraced her mother.

"Let's go inside," I said, ushering both women to the back door of Peg's house. "I told Addison that Ridge is on the scene. I'll call him now to see what he can tell us."

"Who called you, Mom?" Addison asked.

"No one. Salazar Avila came to the house." She looked at Brix. "With you, right? You told Addy."

"That's right." I put my hand on the small of Addison's back. She didn't dispute my affirmation, nor did she tell her mom that Sam had called her.

"Why don't you sit down?" I led her into the living room and over to the sofa. "You too, Peg."

She nodded and sat beside her daughter. The two clasped hands. "Did you say you were going to make a call?"

"I'll do that now." I returned to the kitchen and saw Kick standing near the door. I motioned for him to come inside when I went out.

"Any new information?" I asked when Ridge picked up.

"Fire marshal is here already. Said he suspects arson."

"Not a surprise. Any word on Murphy's twenty?"

"Nothing new yet. You think he might have had something to do with it?"

"If it's money he's after, then I don't. No insurance company will pay out on arson if one of the owners is suspected of starting the fire."

"It's a total loss, Brix. I know I told you that before, but the place burned to the ground."

"You headed home?"

"Unless there's something else you can think of I need to do here."

"Who's at the winery?" I knew it was as hard for him to be away right now as it was for me.

"My dad flew down. My mom is on her way too."

"That's good—and thanks, Ridge."

"Let me know if something comes up."

I told him I would, then ended the call. While Addison and her mother lived several blocks from the ocean, I could still feel the humidity from it. In this case, it was cold, just like the Pacific always was. I shivered but wasn't ready to go back inside.

When Ridge said his father flew in, I couldn't help but wish my own father was still alive. I missed him so much, especially at this time of the year.

The harvest, crush, all of it, was more fun when he ran Los Caballeros. Every year, we sponsored a big party, inviting all the workers in the valley, not just our employees. Ridge's family would help. So would Press and Beau's parents.

The year my dad died, the Butler family hosted instead. After that, the wineries in what we called the "far out" region of Paso Robles took turns. This year was supposed to be our year to host. With everything going on, I couldn't see it happening, although I knew my brothers and sister would make sure it did.

I looked up when Addison came outside. "Hey," I said. "What are you doing out here?"

"Looking for you."

When I held out my arms, she stunned me by walking into my embrace. I stroked her hair when she put her head on my chest, and I could feel the dampness of her tears.

"I can't believe it's gone," she cried. "It feels like only a few minutes ago we were there."

"It does." I tightened my arms when she let go of my waist. "Let me hold you another minute," I whispered.

She put her arms back and moved her head so it rested on my heart. "I don't know how I'll ever thank you."

"You're thanking me right now." I put my hand under her chin, raised her face, and touched her lips with mine. I wanted so much more, but for now, this had to be enough. I kissed her lips and the tip of her nose.

"What was that for?"

"It was me saying, 'you're welcome.'"

Addison shivered.

"Are you cold?" I asked.

"A little."

"Let's go inside."

She took a step back, and our eyes met. In hers, I saw so many questions, none of which I could answer right now.

8
Addison

When I walked into the living room, Brix's brothers were there, but I didn't see my mom.

"She said she was going to lie down," said one of them.

"Oh, um, thanks...I'm sorry, I don't remember your name."

He stood. "I'm Salazar, but everyone calls me Snapper."

"Haven't you met my brothers?" Brix asked.

"I'm sure I have, I just..."

"It's okay," said Snapper. "You're exhausted. You should do what your mom did and try to get some rest."

"You're probably right." I looked at Brix, who motioned with his head toward my apartment.

"Come on, let's go." When he held out his hand, I took it. "By the way, this one is Rascon, aka Kick." As he walked past, he smacked his brother's head with his free hand.

"What was that for?" Kick asked.

"Cuz I'm the oldest."

As an only child, I often wondered what it would be like to have siblings. Although I wasn't sure I would've wanted as many as Brix had.

"They're the youngest two, right? The team ropers?"

"Yep." He shook his head. "The little bastards have always been inseparable. I pity the wives they have someday."

"Are any of your brothers married?"

"Nope. We're all bachelors." He winked, and then his expression grew more serious. "I'm sorry about the diner, Addison."

"I can't help but wonder if maybe it wasn't an accident."

He sighed and pulled me close to him before we walked up the stairs. "It wasn't, baby. At least, the fire marshal doesn't think so."

I shuddered.

"Come on. Let's get you inside."

Rather than go in front of me, this time, Brix followed. I could hear him muttering about how dangerous

"Good night, Addison." When Brix turned to go around the sofa, I grabbed his hand.

His eyes opened wide as I pulled him toward the hallway.

"I don't think I'll be able to sleep unless you're with me."

He stopped walking, looked up at the ceiling a second time, and sighed. "I don't think I'll be able to if I am."

"Come on." I tugged harder. "I'll tell you a bedtime story."

"I was hoping for a lullaby."

I looked over my shoulder at him. "Yeah?"

"Whatever it was you were lip-syncing down the driveway."

"That's hardly a lullaby." I pulled the covers back on the side of the bed I always slept on. "Sorry, it's kind of small." I hadn't thought about how Brix's legs would hang off the end of the full-size bed. It was bigger than the sofa at least.

He walked over to where I stood, hands shaking, a thousand butterflies swirling in my stomach.

"Are you sure you want me in here with you?"

"I am."

"I have one more request." His hands cupped my face.

"What?"

"Can I have a kiss good night?"

"You'll have to get in bed and see." I hoped I came off flirty rather than terrified, which I absolutely was. Brix Avila, the man who starred in nearly every fantasy I'd ever had, was about to get into my bed. How could this even be real?

"Okay if I take this off?" he asked, pointing to his sweatshirt.

"Of course."

I stood completely still and watched him pull it over his head, nearly gasping when I saw he didn't have another shirt on under it.

"Your turn."

"Oh, uh…" I tossed the pillow on the bed that I'd been clutching. I didn't even remember picking it up.

"I can turn around if you want. Or go out while you change."

"It's okay."

There was heat in his eyes as he stood still like I had. Was it my imagination, or were his hands clenched like mine had been earlier?

"I, uh, have something on under mine."

He drew a breath in. "The tank top?"

I nodded but otherwise didn't move.

"Let me see it, baby." He leaned forward and put one knee on the edge of the bed.

I grabbed the hem with both hands and pulled it over my head.

He put his hand on my headboard. "Now the jeans."

"Isn't it your turn?"

"You have something on under yours, right?"

"Yes."

"I don't."

I closed my eyes, feeling light-headed, thinking about Brix being naked under my sheets.

"Addison, at this rate, it'll be sunrise before we even get into bed."

I unfastened the button, pulled down the zipper, and eased the denim over my hips. While I'd left the tank top on under my sweatshirt, I'd taken the boy shorts off and put on panties before I got dressed earlier.

"Jesus," Brix groaned. "Do you have any idea how hard it's going to be for me to keep my hands to myself?"

"Why would you do that?"

"Get in bed. Now, Addison."

I lay down and pulled the sheet over me, waiting, wondering what Brix would do next.

He lay down too but on top of the sheet and with his jeans still on. "Safer this way," he mumbled.

Admittedly, I was disappointed, but what had I expected to happen? Had I really thought that Brix and I would have sex? God, what an idiot I was. I clutched the sheet to my chest and rolled to my side so my back was to him, praying I would be able to stop myself from crying.

"Addison, turn around and look at me."

I shook my head. "Good night."

The bed creaked when he scooted closer and wrapped his arm around me. He moved my hair from the back of my neck with his other hand and kissed right below my ear. "Take your glasses off."

I closed my eyes and practically ripped them from my face. At least he couldn't see how my cheeks flushed in embarrassment. When I was really tired, sometimes I fell asleep with them still on.

"Turn around and let me look at you."

"Brix—"

He turned me when I didn't, so I was flat on my back. The room was dark, but I could still see the way his eyes trailed over my body when he moved the sheet away.

"You're trembling." He put his hand on my abdomen. "Tell me, baby."

I looked into his eyes, wishing my stomach was flatter, tighter, not so fleshy. "Tell you what?"

"When you got to work every day, did you hope I'd come in?"

I nodded.

"Say it."

"Yes, I did."

He smiled. "Close enough." He put his finger on my chin and turned my head so I was facing him. "Now, about that kiss good night…" As he lowered his head, his eyes bored into mine. "I'm not saying you're welcome with this one, Addison. This one means please."

I closed my eyes and waited for the moment when Brix would finally give me a real kiss. The kind I'd fantasized about for years. I could feel his breath, knew he was close, but nothing happened. I raised my lids, and he smiled.

"Your lips have driven me crazy for so long. I want to savor this moment. I also want to be able to look into your mesmerizing eyes."

I was in near agony, waiting for him to move the fraction of an inch that separated us. I expected him to go slow, but he didn't. He crushed his mouth into mine, pushing his tongue through my parted lips. I'd never, ever been kissed like this. Not that I'd been kissed a lot, but even in my wildest dreams, it was never this passionate.

His tongue swirled around mine, and he angled his head, going deeper, pressing harder. Then he eased off, licking the lips he'd just ravished, his tongue slow dancing with mine. All the while, his eyes stayed open, fixated on mine. He eased away and scattered kisses on my face and neck. I waited for him to move lower, to touch my breasts, but he didn't. Instead, he turned and lay on his back, like I was.

"Better than I ever imagined," he murmured, taking my hand and weaving our fingers together. "And believe me, I imagined it often." From the corner of my eye, I could see him turn his head, studying me. "What about you? Did you imagine us kissing?"

"Dreamed of it."

Brix's face broke into a wide smile. Sometime in the last few hours, I'd gotten accustomed to it, so when he did, I wasn't so surprised, but I loved seeing it.

"I dream about you too." He rubbed his eyes with both hands. "We need to sleep. Tomorrow…I guess it's today, is going to be a long one."

"Okay." I was about to turn my back to him again when he told me to sit up. I did, and he tucked his arm under me, pulling me to him. I rested my head on his chest, and he trailed his fingers up and down my arm. That was how I fell asleep.

9
Brix

Even after I was sure Addison had drifted off, I was unable to do the same. Instead of thinking about the diner or her stepfather or even what dawn would bring, I couldn't get my mind off a conversation I'd overheard between her and Sam one afternoon during the summer. I'd had a meeting in San Luis Obispo. Instead of taking the turnoff on Highway 46 and returning to Los Cab, I continued north on Pacific Coast Highway until I reached Cambria.

The garage doors that separated the patio from the inside were wide open, and music was playing louder than usual. I remembered checking my watch and it being close to three. I doubted many customers came in that early, so it didn't surprise me when neither one of them came out from where I could hear them talking in the kitchen. I'd gone to the swinging door to let them know I was there when I heard Sam ask where Addison would go if she could leave tomorrow and money was no object.

"I know it sounds silly," she'd responded. "But I'd go to Big Sur." I recalled being intrigued, given it was less than two hours north of where we were.

"There's this place right on the cliffs that rents tree houses by the night, except they're like no other you've ever seen. They're luxurious, with views of the ocean. And you can get in-house massages."

"I've heard about that place. I also heard it costs three thousand bucks to spend one night there."

"You said if money wasn't an object." I could still hear Addison's rich laughter. It wasn't something I'd heard often enough.

"Exactly. You'll just have to find a wealthy guy to take you."

"Right after I get struck by lightning."

"It could happen."

I never forgot what she'd said next. It hurt my heart to think about now.

"No rich guy would notice me. I'm invisible. And even if he did, it wouldn't be to take me to a three-thousand-dollar-a-night tree house. Maybe to fetch him a cup of coffee."

Sam had laughed. "Or a glass of wine."

I had no idea, then or now, why Addison believed any man, rich or poor, wouldn't notice her. She was gorgeous. Rather than being nothing but skin and bones, she was curvy—more Marilyn Monroe than Cindy Crawford.

Lying next to her now, it was all I could do not to sink into her pillowy softness and ravish the rest of her body like I had her lips. I glanced at her voluptuous breasts, pressed against me, imagining burying my face between them. My cock, now hard as steel, couldn't wait to sink into her hot, wet pussy. When that happened, I'd show her she was anything but invisible.

I closed my eyes tight, telling myself for the thousandth time that this was not how I wanted it to be when Addison and I made love for the first time.

I conjured the tree houses she'd told Sam about and pictured her spread naked before me. I'd shelter her body from the cool ocean breezes with the heat of mine.

When I'd left Stave that afternoon without seeing either Addison or Sam—or having the glass of wine I'd come in for—I drove north for another two hours until I came to the place she'd been talking about.

I was familiar with it, not that I'd ever stayed there, but they'd served our wine since before my father died.

When I asked the GM for a tour of the accommodations, he was more than happy to give it.

He led me out to several of the free-standing structures, built on stilts nine feet off the forest floor and nestled between towering pines.

When we climbed the stairs and walked into the triangular-shaped room, I found it far more luxurious than I'd envisioned, even though Addison had said they were.

There was a king-size bed, fireplace, and window seat as well as an outdoor deck with a view of the ocean.

"Look up," the man had said, pointing to the skylight above the bed. "Best place in the world to watch the stars."

After showing me the tub, triangular-shaped like the house, he rattled off the list of amenities, none of which I paid much attention to until he mentioned an in-room couple's massage—the same one Addison spoke of—followed by a private dinner for two.

I knew now this would be the date I'd offer in the bachelor auction. The one I intended to make sure Addison won—I didn't care how much it cost me to get Alex to go along with it. In fact, I'd already decided

I'd tack an extra fifty grand on whatever the bid was, just to make sure everything went as I planned. My sister didn't know it, but every year I'd refused to be in the auction, it was the amount I donated instead.

With the dream of Addison and me in that tree house, our naked bodies pleasuring each other, was how I finally drifted to sleep.

I was stunned when I rolled over and saw the clock read ten. I couldn't remember a time in my life when I'd slept so late. My exhaustion, coupled with the warmth of Addison's body next to mine, had to be the reason.

At some point, she'd turned so her back was to me. I'd turned too, nestling her against my front, where my hardness—albeit through my jeans—now rested between the cheeks of her ass.

As much as I longed to strip her of her clothes and wake her with my mouth on her pussy, the fantasy of that happening for the first time in the tree house she'd dreamed of spending the night in, kept a tight hold on my resolve.

I reached behind me and grabbed my phone, pleasantly surprised there were no calls or messages. My plan for today was to find out what I could about the fire as well as talk to Alex about the bachelor auction. One of the stipulations of me agreeing to be in it was that the details of the date be kept a secret, even after the gavel fell on the winning bid.

The way the announcement of the winner was handled was yet another stipulation. No one could know it was Addison. My sister had to agree it remained anonymous. In exchange, I would allow her to tag the extra fifty grand onto whatever that bid was and announce it as the final amount.

I knew her well enough to be confident she'd go along with it. It meant the gauntlet would be thrown down for next year's highest bid to exceed that number.

Addison groaned, and I watched as she opened her eyes and shielded them from the sun streaming in the bedroom window. She peeked over her shoulder at me.

"Good morning, baby." I leaned forward and kissed her.

"How long have you been awake?" she asked.

"A few minutes."

She shifted to her back and closed her eyes.

"Go back to sleep," I whispered.

"The diner…"

I kissed her forehead like I had her lips. "Whatever needs to be done can wait."

I tucked the blanket around her and waited until I was sure she was asleep before easing myself off the bed. I used the restroom, put my sweatshirt and shoes back on, and crept out the front door, making sure it wasn't locked before closing it behind me.

My plan was to grab the overnight bag from the truck and get back upstairs before Addison woke again. When I saw Ridge sitting on the front stoop of Peg's house, I knew it wouldn't be that simple.

"Hey," I said, walking up and putting my hand on the porch rail.

Ridge looked in my direction and lowered his sunglasses. "Good morning." He glanced at his phone. "Not that there's much left of it."

"What's up?"

He handed me an envelope. "Surveillance photos from last night."

"From where?" I didn't remember seeing any cameras at the diner.

"Inn next door," he said as I opened the envelope and pulled out the first image.

"Holy shit." The photo of a man holding a gasoline can was as clear as if it had been taken with a zoom lens. However, his face was hidden. I pulled out the rest and looked through them, but in every one, the man's face was obscured.

"Think it could be Murphy?" Ridge asked.

"Impossible to tell." I flipped through them a second time. "What about the sheriff? Does he have any clue as to who it might be?"

"Don't know yet." He motioned with his head to the envelope. "Vader doesn't know I have those."

Conrad Krouse, the local sheriff, had been given the nickname of the Star War's character because of how loud his breathing sounded on the other end of a phone call.

"Where'd you get them?"

"MaryBeth."

The eighty-year-old woman owned the inn next to the diner. "You're a scoundrel."

"It only cost me a bouquet of flowers and bottle of your wine."

"Nice."

Ridge looked behind us and up at the apartment. "How's Addy?"

"Hopefully back to sleep."

He studied me but didn't say anything.

"What?"

"You sure about this, Brix?"

I looked up at the trees.

"She hasn't had an easy life. You know that as well as I do. This shit with her stepfather and the fire only makes it worse. I don't see it getting easier anytime soon."

I glared at him. "What's your point?"

"Now might not be the best time to start something with her. Especially…"

At times in my life, I'd wanted to kick the ass of the man in front of me. Not very many and none more than right now. "Especially, what?" I spat.

"You aren't exactly one whose interest is held for very long, my friend."

"Maybe she's different. You think of that? Maybe I'm different."

"If you need to throw more than one 'maybe' out there, I'd say you better make sure you *are* different before you do something you'll regret." He took his glasses off. "Or is it already too late?"

"What it is, is none of your fucking business."

"I wish I could apologize, but I've seen it one too many times with you. If you hurt her, I'll make it my business. I won't be the only one who does, either."

"What the hell, Ridge? Do you really believe I'd do that?"

"I'm not sure what to think."

"Think this. I've been crazy about Addison for as long as I can remember. If you haven't noticed that, you're as blind as you are stupid."

"I know you have. How long will it last, though, once she's no longer a challenge?"

"You're out of line."

"I hope you're right."

I shook my head and walked away. I didn't need to explain myself to Ridge, best friend or not. Addison wasn't a fucking challenge to me. Only when I got to the top of the stairs did I remember why I'd gone down in the first place. Rather than subjecting myself to more of Ridge's shit, I'd wait and get my clothes later.

When I opened the front door, Addison was standing in the living room. "I thought you'd left."

"Nope. Just went outside for a minute."

She studied me, and I wondered if she'd ask why. Her only question was whether I'd seen her mom.

"I didn't. Ridge stopped by for a minute to say he was heading to the winery."

"Do you need to go too?"

Probably, but for now I was needed here more. "Maybe later."

"I should check on her." She looked down at what she was wearing, like she had in the middle of the night. "After I get dressed."

Part of me wanted to follow her down the hallway and help her, but I was in this for a much longer haul. It wouldn't be easy, but I was adamant that the first time I had my body wrapped around Addison's naked one, we'd be in a tree house overlooking the ocean.

As much as I wanted to keep them away from the place where the diner no longer stood, Peg was insistent she had to meet her insurance agent there.

Both Addison and I tried to tell her she could file the claim over the phone, but she refused.

"Matt asked me to."

I'd gone to high school with Matt Conseco, who'd taken over the family's insurance agency when his father retired. When the opportunity presented itself, I'd let him know exactly what I thought about him requiring his client to meet him at the scene the day after the fire happened.

When we pulled into the parking lot, I saw another close friend, winemaker, *and* my attorney, Zin Oliver, talking to Matt and Vader. A man I didn't recognize approached them. When he did, Zin walked toward my truck.

I stopped and parked, but by the time I got around to the passenger side, Peg had gotten out. I held my hand out for Addison.

She murmured her thanks, but she wasn't looking at me. Her gaze was focused on the charred remains of the place that was as much a part of this community as any winery had ever been.

As Ridge had said, the structure had burned right to the ground, aided by an accelerant we could now assume was gasoline.

I watched Peg walk in Matt's direction, relieved when I saw Zin intercept her. I put my hand on the small of Addison's back and led her to where they stood.

"I don't understand," I heard Peg say as we approached.

"What's going on, Mom? Hey, Zin."

"Hey, Addy. I was just telling your mom there appears to be evidence that the fire wasn't accidental."

Addison nodded.

"You knew already?" Peg asked, looking between her daughter and me.

"I had a hard time believing it was," she responded, stepping forward to put her hand around her mother's shoulders. "Brix said the fire marshal suspected arson."

"Oh my God." Peg put her hand in front of her mouth. "Who would do something like this?"

I motioned Zin off to the side. "Who's the guy in the dark jacket."

"Insurance investigator."

"That was quick."

"No kidding. Matt's the one who called and asked me to come down here. He was surprised by it too."

"You think Vader contacted him?"

"First question I asked when he walked over to my SUV before I was even out of it, wanting to know why I showed up."

"What did he say?"

"He said it seemed unusual to him."

"Maybe the fire marshal contacted him."

"It's the only logical explanation, but if that were the case, I'd expect to see law enforcement here."

"What's he want?"

"I haven't talked to him yet, but according to Vader, he wants to question Peg and Addy."

"What's your legal opinion on that?"

"Not without counsel present."

"Are you offering to represent them, Zin?"

"Get them both to give me a dollar, Brix."

I nodded and walked over to Addison, whispering what I wanted her to do and why. "Your mom too, okay?"

She nodded like I had, and when I saw the two approach Zin, I walked over to Matt and Vader.

"Hey, Brix," said Matt. "How're Peg and Addy holding up?"

"Been a rough night." I turned to the investigator and held out my hand. "I'm Gabriel Avila."

"Paul Stevens with Mutual Life."

"You the adjuster?"

He shook his head. "Investigator."

I looked at Matt. "Have you filed a claim already?"

"I haven't."

I turned back to Stevens. "Who called you out here?"

He cleared his throat. "That isn't any of your business."

"What's that?" asked Zin, walking up and putting his hand on my shoulder.

"I asked who called him here."

Zin handed the man a card. "Allow me to introduce myself. I'm Vail Oliver, and I'll be representing Margaret Murphy and Addison Reagan."

Addison tapped me on the shoulder, and I took a step away from the other men.

"I did what you asked, but do I really need Zin to represent me? I don't have anything to do with this."

"The investigator wants to ask both you and your mother a few questions. It's best to have legal advice during that process."

She nodded and crossed her arms.

"Are you cold? Would you rather wait in the truck?"

"If you don't mind."

"Come on." I'd parked in such a way that I was facing the ocean rather than where the diner once stood. I opened her door, Addison climbed in, and I went around to the other side. I started the engine and turned up the heat. "Scoot over here and let me warm you up."

"I'm okay."

"All right, then. Scoot on over here and warm me up. I'm the one with nothing on under my sweatshirt."

She rolled her eyes at me like she had when we worked together a few hours ago. It only made me want to flirt with her more—then and now. Looking in the rearview mirror, I couldn't believe the diner was gone. Yesterday had been one of the best days I could remember.

As much as I was needed at Los Cab, I'd been looking forward to another day spent just like the one before.

I peered over at Addison, who was still sitting too far away, and found her studying me.

"Something you want to ask me?"

"What did you mean when you said you'd be in the auction but you had stipulations?"

I just grinned.

"And one relates to me?"

"It does. The only way I'll do it is if you make the winning bid on me."

Addison's mouth opened and closed. It opened again, and she shook her head. "I can't figure out if you're trying to be funny or you're just an asshole."

I slid over, intending to reveal my plan, but when I tried to put my arm around her, Addison opened the passenger door, got out, and slammed it behind her.

10
Addison

"Wait!" I heard him call after me, but I kept walking. There were a lot of words I'd used to describe Brix, but cruel had never been one of them. Suggesting the only way he'd be in the auction was if I was the winning bidder—something he knew was impossible, given I literally had *no* money—was downright mean.

"Leave me alone, Brix!" I shouted behind me.

His hand clamped on my shoulder, and his arm snaked around my waist. "Hear me out."

I wrenched out of his grasp. "Why didn't you just say no? See? This is why I didn't want to ask you. God, I can't believe this. And to think—"

"Will you please listen?"

"No. You're—" I stopped talking when Brix picked me up and tossed me over his shoulder. *"What are you doing?"*

"Taking you somewhere where you'll have to let me explain."

"*What?* Where?"

"I haven't figured that out yet."

I pounded on his back. "Put me down, dammit!"

"Only if you agree to hear me out."

"Okay, I'll hear you out." When he set me on my feet, I folded my arms and glared at him.

"You *bid,* but I *pay*. It's the only way I'll agree to it."

"I don't understand. Why do it at all, then?"

"Because everyone gets what they want. Alex will be happy because I'm finally in the auction. I'm happy because I get to have a date with you. Earlier, I might have said you'd be happy for the same reason. Best of all, Children's Hospital gets a minimum of fifty grand. Probably more."

I had to admit, at least inwardly, that it was a very sweet thing for him to do. "I'm sorry." I said it so quietly I wasn't sure he heard.

"What was that?" When he grinned, I knew he had.

"You heard me."

"What are you sorry for, Addison?"

"For thinking you were making fun of me."

"I would never do that to you." He looked up at the sky and shook his head. "First Ridge, now you."

"What are you talking about?"

He looked down at me with the same look of vulnerability I'd seen on his face before, when he confessed he came to Stave just to see me. "He warned me not to hurt you. I couldn't believe he thought I would."

"And I just did the same thing."

When Brix put his hands on my shoulders and I put mine on his waist, he smiled. "I can't promise I won't say something stupid, like I did a few minutes ago, but I can promise I'll never say or do anything at your expense."

"I'm sorry I reacted the way I did. Overreacted is more like it. It's just that growing up here, *everyone* had more money than my mom and I did. It's something I've always been self-conscious about. Plus, this—meaning you and me—isn't immediately obvious to anyone." I motioned with my head to where my mother, the sheriff, our insurance agent, and one of Brix's best friends were all looking in our direction.

I dropped my hands, expecting him to do the same. Instead, he moved one hand to my neck, put the other arm around my waist, pulled me into him, and kissed me. Not a short, chaste kiss. It was long and full of passion. He didn't let go when the kiss ended, either.

"I want you to know something else, Addison," he murmured against the top of my head. "That kiss wasn't for them; it was for you."

I sneaked a look over at our audience. Only Zin was still looking in our direction, and he waved us over.

"About time you made a move," I heard him mumble to Brix when we got closer and he came to meet us partway. "I have an update."

"Go ahead," said Brix.

"The investigator received an anonymous tip from someone who saw Dennis Murphy torching the place last night."

"Did Vader tell him there was security footage?"

Zin looked as stunned as I was. "Yeah, but how did you know there was?"

"Ridge had a date with MaryBeth earlier this morning."

Zin laughed, and Brix leaned closer to me when my eyes opened wide. "He had a hunch she might have security cameras directed at the diner. In exchange for a copy of last night's footage, he brought her a bouquet of flowers and a bottle of wine."

"Was it him?" I whispered.

"Impossible to tell from what I saw. I don't know if Vader has more than that."

"When's the last time you saw your stepfather?" Zin asked.

"Two mornings ago. At the diner."

"What about later in the day?"

I shook my head. "What did my mom say?"

"Pretty much the same thing. She said he left straight from there to help some out-of-town family member with a remodel."

"Addison has reason to believe he didn't leave right away."

Zin nodded. "I see. Let's not get into it here, then. Is there somewhere else we can talk?"

"With my mom or not?"

"Not," he said, looking over at her, then back at me. "What happened to her arm?"

"We'll talk more about that at Addison's apartment. Okay with you?" Brix asked me.

"That's fine."

"Since Stevens isn't officially law enforcement, I told him to contact my office about scheduling a meeting for him to talk to you and your mother."

"What about Vader?"

"Let's just say Murphy isn't his favorite person." Zin pulled out his phone. "I'd rather your mother not know we're meeting, and my guess is you'd prefer it that way too. Instead of getting together at your apartment, how about Stave around one o'clock? Sound good?"

It was perfect since the wine bar didn't open until four. "It's Tuesday," I gasped. "I'm supposed to work today."

"What time is that?" asked Brix.

"Two." I looked over at Zin.

"We should be done long before that."

"Addison, I'm sure Alex or Sam can work for you today," said Brix after we waved goodbye to Zin and were walking over to my mother, who was still talking to the sheriff and our insurance guy.

"I'd rather work. Plus, don't you need to get back to Los Cab?"

"I probably should."

"Ready, Mom?" I asked, motioning with my head toward Brix's truck.

"Conrad is going to give me a ride back to the house. You two go on ahead."

"Is that a good idea?" I asked Brix while I waited for him to open the passenger door.

"If you mean because he's the sheriff, my answer is no. Otherwise, yes."

I cocked my head. "I don't understand."

"You know how you thought you and I weren't immediately obvious? Take a gander at Vader sometime when your mom's around."

I looked over to where she stood, waiting for the sheriff to open the front passenger door of his unmarked car. I might not have noticed if Brix hadn't pointed it out, but when Vader said something, my mother laughed. How long had it been since I'd even seen her smile around her husband? I couldn't recall.

"I wish he was her type," I murmured.

Brix leaned in close and kissed my forehead. "Why wouldn't he be?"

"My mom is only attracted to the bad ones."

He laughed and held out his hand to help me into his truck. I was perfectly capable of getting in on my own, but I loved that he was such a gentleman about it.

"I hope it isn't like mother, like daughter," he said after he'd gotten in the driver's side and started the engine.

"Oh no. I'm the exact opposite." I looked at him and smiled. "I only go for the good guys."

"I will always be that for you, Addison. No matter what."

"That's quite a statement, Brix."

"I mean every word."

I watched as he took out his phone and tapped the screen. When he reached over and turned the volume up on the stereo and "Trees" started to play, it was an acoustic version I'd never heard before. It sounded as if the lead singer was being accompanied by an orchestra.

"This version sounds like a lullaby." He smiled.

"Maybe I'll lip-sync it to you sometime."

"I'd rather you sing it."

I rested my head against the back of the seat and laughed. "You haven't heard me sing."

"Sure, I have."

I studied him. "When?"

"I've heard you and Sam. You have a much better voice than she does, by the way."

"How do you know she isn't the one with the better voice?"

Brix shifted so his body was facing mine. "I just know."

I looked at the time on my phone. We were supposed to meet Zin at Stave in less than an hour. Before that, I'd need to shower and get ready. I'd told Brix I'd prefer to work, but I was exhausted just thinking about it.

That really wasn't anything new. Exhaustion was a regular part of my life. I couldn't remember the last time I'd had an entire day off. Not since my mom bought the diner. To be fair, she hadn't had a day off, either.

As heartbreaking as it was that the Olallieberry Diner and Bakery was gone—it had been a mainstay of the community for years—maybe the fire was a blessing, especially if the insurance paid off the money she'd borrowed against her house to buy it. She'd still have to get another job; I just hoped it didn't involve working so many hours.

When Brix pulled up in front of my mom's place, a feeling of dread came over me. I was sure Dennis would reappear at any moment, and I had no idea what to expect when he did.

The other thing I dreaded was that soon Brix would have to leave and return to his life. He'd put it on hold for me for almost forty-eight hours and at the worst possible time of the year for the winery.

"What's goin' on, Addison?" he asked.

I turned in my seat so I could look him in the eye. "I want you to know how much I appreciate all the help you've given me. I mean, just even being here…" I hated that I was about to cry. I did so easily when I was tired.

"Sounds like you're saying goodbye, but I know that can't be."

"So long?"

"I'm not leaving, baby."

When I rolled my eyes, Brix raised an eyebrow. "Sorry," I muttered. "And you'll have to leave at some point. You know, go back to making wine and all that. Maybe finish crush. Those remaining grapes aren't just going to hang out on the vine, waiting on you."

He laughed. "Alex called in reinforcements. For all I know, we're done."

"You're joking, right?"

He shook his head. "Maddox and Naughton Butler showed up yesterday afternoon. Last I heard, there were three vineyards Naught thought were ready. Since I haven't heard from Enzo, either nothing else is, or they've decided they don't need to run it by me."

"How do you feel about that?"

He rested his head against the back of his seat. "Honestly? Relieved. When Ridge said his father flew down from Napa, it made me realize how much I miss my dad. I mean, I miss him all the time, but especially at this time of the year. Just having someone to walk the vineyards with would be nice."

"What about one of your brothers?"

He shrugged his shoulder. "I've tried to get Enzo to step up, but he hasn't."

"You just said you haven't heard from him. Maybe he is now."

"Maybe. Or Naught is making all the decisions, and Enzo is just going along with it."

"If you feel like you need to get back, I can handle talking to Zin."

Brix reached over and put his hand on mine. "What if I told you I don't want to leave?"

"Well, I really wouldn't be *that* surprised. I'm sure my apartment is way nicer than wherever you live. Not to mention, there isn't a bed made that is more comfortable than mine. You remember? The one where your feet hang off the end."

He laughed. "Come on, let's get you inside."

I laughed out loud. "Since when?"

"Since always. You've just never taken time off."

I bit my bottom lip, hating to point out the obvious. "I make a lot in tips, Alex."

"See, that's the thing. Stave makes up the difference if you're out sick, err, or for another good reason."

I rolled my eyes, this time not at all apologetic for it. "That's a flat-out lie."

"Who cares? I own the place. I make the rules. You can't come back to work until I say so. Oh, and tell my brother we don't need him at Los Cab, either."

Brix was leaning against the side of his truck and gave me a thumbs-up.

"Alrighty, then, I'll see you at two unless you're already gone by then."

"Alex, come on, what about Coco?"

"Neither one of her *abuelas* will hand her over anyway, so I might as well work."

11
Brix

I couldn't get a read on whether Addison intended to accept Alex's offer to take her shift or if once she got to Stave, she'd want to stay. Either way, my plan was to drive her there and make sure she got home okay.

A few minutes ago, I'd received a text from Kick, saying he and Snapper were at Peg's house, had done a sweep of both the main residence and the apartment, and planned to surveil the property for the night.

Addison and I were walking up the driveway when Vader pulled up. By the look on his face as well as Peg's, I knew something else must've happened.

"Hang on," I said to Addison, who was almost to the steps of her apartment.

When I walked over to the sheriff's car and was about to open the passenger door to help Addison's mother out, Vader made eye contact and shook his head.

"The house has been cleared," I told him when he closed the door behind him and we walked a few feet away from the car.

"Brix, we've talked about this before. You and the rest of your vigilantes can't take on the role of law enforcement just because you think you're entitled to."

Vader was one of the only people outside of current and past members aware of Los Caballeros' existence. While he was cautioning me now, there were times in the past when he'd come to us for help.

"Are you telling me you have the manpower to run teams of two twenty-four seven?"

"You know I don't."

"Then, let us do what we do. Now, tell me what has you and Peg so shaken."

Vader pulled a cell out of his pocket and handed it to me. There was a photo loaded on the screen. "Pay up or the house is next," had been scrawled in the ash covering the former diner's concrete slab.

"You don't appear surprised."

I looked from the phone to him. "I'm not."

"You wanna fill me in on what you know and why you didn't think it was important to read me in?"

I wanted to suggest to Vader that he was being mighty hypocritical, given less than a couple of minutes ago, he'd informed me that the rest of my vigilantes and me shouldn't take on the role of law enforcement, but now wasn't the time to get into a pissing match with the sheriff.

"Press looked into Murphy's background. I guess the first thing you should know is that isn't his real name, although we haven't been able to find out what is. He operates under at least one other alias—Patrick Sullivan." I looked over at the car, then to Addison, who stood in the driveway. "Maybe we should get Peg inside before we continue this conversation."

Vader nodded and returned to his vehicle while I joined Addison near the steps to her mother's porch.

"What's going on?" she asked.

I put my arm around her shoulders and pulled her close, wishing I could wait until we were alone to tell her about the words scrawled in the diner's ashes. However, Vader and Peg were headed our way. If I didn't tell Addison, her mother certainly would.

"Someone left a message at the scene of the fire. We believe it may have been meant for Murphy."

"What did it say?"

I told her the words I'd read on Vader's phone and turned her toward me when she gasped and put her hand in front of her mouth.

"Look at me, baby." I waited for her eyes to meet mine. "We're going to keep you, your mom, and her house safe. I want you to know that."

She nodded but, otherwise, didn't respond.

"Addy?" Peg called out.

I released her, and she rushed over to her mom. "Brix told me," I heard her say as the two embraced.

"Conrad believes it was a message for Dennis," Peg told her daughter.

"Let's go inside," Vader suggested, his eyes roaming the area in the same way mine were.

"Good idea." I went to the door first and waited for Peg to hand me her keys. "Before we go in, I want you to know my brothers checked the house and apartment a few minutes before we arrived."

Neither woman commented. The shock of the threat obviously far outweighed my words.

I had no idea what "Conrad," as Peg had called him, was thinking, but I had already begun formulating a plan involving Addison—one I hoped she'd consent to.

"Mom? Can I get you anything?" When Peg didn't answer, Addison repeated her words.

"I'm sorry, what did you say?"

"I asked if I could get you anything."

"No. I'm fine. Thanks."

Something was off. Peg's answer sounded like she was speaking to a polite stranger.

Addison squeezed my hand, then sat down next to her on the sofa when her mom took a seat.

"Brix, I think it would be best if you told Peg and Addy what you confided in me a few minutes ago."

I didn't agree, but Vader left me little choice. I walked over, sat in the chair closest to the sofa, and leaned forward.

"A friend of mine—you both know him—Press Barrett, did some digging into Dennis Murphy's background." Peg raised her head, her eyes scrunched. "The first thing you should know is that Murphy is an alias."

I looked over at Vader, wondering if he was as confused by Peg's lack of reaction as I was. Suddenly, it was as though she came out of a stupor.

"What are you talking about?" Peg asked, looking first at me, then Vader, then at her daughter.

"But they're married," said Addison. "Is that even legal?"

He sat and leaned forward in the same way I had. "It depends. In the State of California, a spouse may request an annulment if they were unaware of their partner's real name."

Addison turned toward me. "What is his real name?"

"We aren't certain, but he has another known alias—Patrick Sullivan."

She repeated the name under her breath. "What else did Press find out about him?"

"We believe he's in a great deal of debt—from gambling." Like with everything else I'd divulged so far, I had no desire to continue. I had to, though. "There is also evidence he recently took out a life insurance policy. Were you aware of that, Peg?"

She shook her head. I couldn't figure out if she was stunned or if something else was going on.

Addison's forehead scrunched. "On who?"

"Your mom, baby," I answered, reaching for her hand.

She closed her eyes and breathed deeply before turning to her mother. "You didn't fall down the stairs, did you?"

Peg's eyes filled with tears. "I did, Addy."

"Wait. He *pushed* you?"

"We were arguing—"

"And he pushed you down the stairs?"

Shouting at her mother was doing neither woman any good. I stood, moved to the sofa, and sat beside Addison, then put my arm around her. "Let's focus on our next steps," I whispered.

Her eyes met mine. "What else have you found out about him?"

"He may have been spotted in Mojave."

"May have been?"

"That's right. And for that reason, I want to suggest you stay elsewhere for a few days at least."

"They wrote, 'Pay up or the house is next.' You said a great deal of debt. What does that mean?"

First of all, I wasn't certain of the exact figure. Second, would knowing what Press believed it to be do her any good? "A significant amount."

"How much, Brix?" Addison pressed.

"We have no verifiable evidence, but we're estimating at least a couple of hundred thousand."

"Oh my God!" It was the first significant reaction I'd seen out of Peg, who turned an alarming shade of pale. "There is no way in the world I can pay that."

"No one is suggesting you do," said Vader. "We'll do everything in our power to keep your house safe while we hunt down Murphy—or whatever the hell his name is."

As far as hunting down Murphy, aka Sullivan, I had other ideas. However, under no circumstances could Vader be made aware of any of it.

"What if you can't find him?" Addison asked.

"We will," Vader and I answered at the same time.

"I'd like you both to come stay at Los Cab," I added. "There's plenty of room, and you'll be safe there."

We didn't need to decide now, but I'd prefer Addison stay with me. I'd understand, though, if she wanted to be with her mom. In fact, until I was able to put certain things in place, that's where I'd need her to be.

I'd anticipated both women's reluctance to stay at our family's ranch as well as their argument that doing so would bring danger to our door. While I couldn't divulge much of anything about the security put in place there by one of the world's best in intelligence technology—a neighbor, in fact—Vader and I were persuasive enough that they gave in.

"I'll ask Zin to come to Los Cab later this afternoon rather than meet at Stave," I told Addison when we went up to her apartment so she could pack a few things.

"Probably for the best." Her eyes were downcast, and she looked on the verge of tears.

I gathered her in my arms. "We'll get through this. I promise."

She pulled back and studied me. "This isn't yours to get through, Brix. I appreciate everything you're doing, but—"

I put my fingertips on her lips. "There is nothing you can say or do that will change the fact that I intend to keep the promise I just made."

Addison leaned forward and put her head on my chest. "Thank you," she whispered. "I truly don't know how we'd manage without your help."

I knew it was equally hard to accept—and admit—she needed the help I insisted on giving. However, she had no choice, because I would continue regardless of her acceptance.

"You in my arms is all the thanks I need, baby."

When she raised her head and looked into my eyes, I knew what I needed to say couldn't be conveyed with words. Only lips. It had been too long since I tasted her sweetness.

I tangled her tongue with mine when she opened her mouth to me. While I may have intended to keep our kiss soft and languid, I gave in to the passion instead. How many times had I fantasized about making Addison Reagan mine? I'd lost count. It didn't matter anyway, now that it was real.

Her fingers dug into my chest, and she angled her head, kissing me back harder, deeper. When she leaned her pelvis into me, it was impossible to thwart my body's natural response. Not now, I reminded myself. Not like this. When I finally knew how it felt to be buried deep inside the woman who made me burn with desire, I vowed to make at least one of her fantasies come true. She didn't believe anyone would ever whisk her away to her tree house, but I'd prove her wrong.

12
Addison

When the kiss between Brix and I ended and he rested his forehead against mine, I thought about pinching myself. It was as though I spent nearly every moment thinking I'd wake up any minute from the bizarre dreams I was having. Well, some were dreams, fantasies really, while others were nightmares.

It was a toss-up as to which was harder to wrap my head around—what was happening between Brix and me, or the horror of what my mom and I had just learned about her husband. Or was he her husband? I wasn't sure, based on Vader's response to my question.

While my mom appeared to be in shock, I had no idea what the news of Dennis owing hundreds of thousands of dollars in gambling debts meant for her—or me.

Brix obviously believed we were in danger, given he wanted the two of us to stay at Los Caballeros. I couldn't help but worry what would happen if Vader was unable to find Dennis. Surely, whoever he owed the money to would come after my mother, at least. Maybe me too.

Brix pulled back and looked into my eyes. "I know it isn't easy, but please trust what I said about us getting through this, Addison."

I wanted to tell him I *did* trust him, but it wasn't that simple. A little over forty-eight hours ago, he swept into my life and all but took over. He'd insisted on helping at the diner, then spent every minute with me since that morning. More than a whirlwind, it felt like a tornado.

I knew Brix, though. Apart from not being as grumpy as I always found him to be, he was exactly the man I'd hoped he was. Plus, I knew his sister better than I knew him. Alex had always treated me fairly and respectfully. I had no doubt everyone in their family would do the same.

"Addison?" he whispered.

"Yes? Right. I'm sorry. It's just been a helluva two days. Ya know?"

He laughed. "That's one way of putting it." He moved his hand to the back of my neck. "I've always admired your resilience, your tenacity. I wish I could be more like you."

I shook my head. Now I was sure I was dreaming. "You wish you could be more like *me*?"

"I do. As I said, you have a way of taking everything in stride that I wish I possessed. With everything but the winery, I tend to act first and think later. You're the opposite."

I couldn't say whether I agreed or disagreed with Brix's assessment. It wasn't like I had a choice. The responsibilities I had were not the same as his. My life was simple. Get up. Go to work. Go to a different work. Come home. Sleep. Repeat.

He followed me into the bedroom and sat on the bed while I tried to figure out what to pack. "Um, what should I bring? Or…err…how much?"

Brix lay back and rested on his elbows. "If you leave that to me, you'll either bring very little or everything."

I smiled. "What does that mean?"

He stood, walked over, and pulled my body into his. "I'd love to keep you in as few clothes as possible, but then I'd also never want you to leave."

"Brix…I…" His kiss stopped me from continuing and saved me from embarrassment when—after telling him things were moving too fast for me—he assured me he was only joking.

"There is something I need to ask while we're still alone," he said, rubbing my nose with the tip of his. "I have my own place on the ranch. My suggestion is that your mother stay in the main house with my mother and you with me. However, if that would make you uncomfortable, I won't push."

Sure, I'd love to stay with Brix, but would it be wise? Absolutely not. Besides, my mom might feel weird if I wasn't with her.

"I should—" He kissed me again, and I giggled. "Are you going to let me finish?"

"Nope. I know what you're going to say, and I don't want to hear it. While I said I wouldn't push, I didn't say I wouldn't be disappointed."

"Brix?"

"Yeah, baby?"

"How much danger are we in?" I could tell he didn't want to answer, but I had to know.

"As I said, we believe the message was for Murphy. The people who we suspect started the fire at the diner want him to know they aren't going to back down."

"My mom doesn't have that kind of money. She doesn't have *any* to speak of."

"Addison?"

I smiled. "Yeah, baby?"

Brix squeezed me. "Man, I like the sound of that."

"Did you want to ask me something?"

He nodded. "Do you trust me?"

Having just thought it through, answering him was easy. "I do."

"Damn, I don't know which I like better. You saying you trust me without any hesitation or you calling me baby." He pulled me over to sit on the edge of the bed. "I'm going to take care of this, Addison. I need you to trust that I will, and not ask me any questions."

"What are you going to do?"

He smiled, and I rolled my eyes.

"Seriously, you can't expect me to just accept you're going to take care of it without telling me what you plan to do."

"I can expect that if you trust me."

I stared into his eyes. "Okay."

"Once I get you settled at Los Cab, there are a few things I need to take care of. I'm sorry, but I may be gone for a couple of hours."

"Of course. I mean, I know you have so many things to do that have nothing to do with me. Please don't feel like you have to apologize, and please don't feel like

"My father wanted to build a more modern place for them to live in once all of us kids moved out, but my mother wouldn't hear of it."

"I wouldn't have, either," I murmured, looking over the seat at my own mom and wishing she didn't look so sad. I hated Dennis even more for putting her through everything he had. The woman deserved so much better. Like a husband who would want to build her a new house, but would acquiesce when she said she liked the one she had. I wished so much she had found a man like that.

"You're here!" I heard Brix's mother shout and saw her rushing in our direction. Rather than wait for Brix to come around and open my door, I got out so he could help my mother instead.

She was barely out of the backseat of the truck's cab before Mrs. Avila was at her side.

"We've got this. Go do what you need to do," I told Brix after he brought our bags inside and showed us to what I thought was our room. It had two twin beds and a nightstand in between.

"Hang on, I need to ask my mother which room she got ready for you."

"My mom and I can share."

"Lunch is ready!" his mother called out from the kitchen before Brix could respond. Whatever she'd made smelled divine. My stomach rumbled in appreciation, making me realize I had no idea the last time I ate anything. Brix either.

"I know I just told you to go do what you need to, but first you have to eat."

Brix smiled. "I do?"

I nodded. "When was your last meal or even snack?"

His eyes were focused on mine, but I could tell he was trying to remember. "Damn. I think it was at the diner."

He pulled me around the corner and into the kitchen, where I saw Mrs. Avila had made Santa Maria-style tri-tip sandwiches, baked beans, coleslaw, and potato salad.

I was hungry enough that when Brix went back for seconds and refilled my plate at the same time, I dug in.

"Save room for dessert," Mrs. Avila said as I took my last bite of sandwich.

"I can't eat another thing, but thank you," I said, standing to take Brix's plate and mine to the sink.

"Not to worry. I'll pack a to-go box. What's your favorite, Addy? Apple or cherry pie?"

"Cherry," my mother answered for me.

"My Gabe too," Mrs. Avila said with a wink. "I'll just send the whole pie with them, then. I'll make another for us, Peg."

I looked between her and Brix. "I'm…um…staying here."

"Don't be silly. I have seven grown children, *mija*. I know you two would rather be on your own than hang out with your *madres*."

Brix walked over and put his arm around her. "I have a couple of errands to run. I'm going to trust you'll take care of Addison while I'm gone."

She put her head on his shoulder. "My Gabe is a sweet man, but he works too much. Just like his papa."

"Walk me out?" Brix asked.

"I'll let her know I'm going to stay here," I said once we were on the porch.

He shook his head. "You heard her. We'd rather be on our own. At least, I would."

The kiss he gave me made me rethink my earlier decision. "Let me talk to my mom first."

13

Brix

I'd asked Ridge to contact the rest of the Caballeros and have them meet inside the wine caves on our ranch as soon as they could get there. The only person I knew wouldn't be joining us was Uncle Trystan.

Since before my aunt passed away last year, the two had spent most of their time at their ranch in Mexico. He still attended our meetings as long as he was given ample notice.

I parked my truck and opened the main gate leading into the part of the caves where we offered tours. Once inside, I used a skeleton key to unlock the door to a rarely used corridor.

In my left hand, I carried a long-handled electric torch to see in the pitch-black walkways. Every few feet, I stopped and used it to light the ancient tempest sconces that illuminated the way to the room where the members of Los Caballeros Society had been meeting since 1769. It was a brisk walk in the musty cavern that stayed an even fifty-five to sixty degrees year-round, the perfect temperature for storing barrels upon barrels of some of the world's best wines.

The Los Cab caves had been dug out from a dusty, rugged hillside deemed unsuitable for vineyard planting back when my ancestors settled in the area. These days, every available hectare was planted with something, including the earth above where I stood.

A single large round wooden table sat amidst the racks that stored the barrels. One by one, the other members of the covert organization walked in and took their designated seat. As was customary, no one spoke until all those expected had arrived.

I nodded my head as I made eye contact with each of the men I considered a brother—whether by blood or not. Those in the room were here because their fathers and grandfathers had been members. It was a rare occurrence when anyone new was invited, and if they were, they had to meet certain criteria.

First, they had to be presented for consideration by an active member. Next, their family had to have been in the wine industry for at least two generations. Third, the prospective member had to be worth a billion dollars or more in their own right. And lastly, they had to agree not to divulge the existence of Los Caballeros and the work we did to anyone outside of our tight-knit circle.

While not a mandate, having a good seat in the saddle was necessary, given the annual one-hundred-mile ride out we did in the spring—a Spanish tradition stemming back to the fourteen hundreds. It was then that the Knights Templar defeated the Moors and took control of a town, Jerez, in southwestern Spain. They renamed it Jerez de los Caballeros—direct translation: Jerez of the Knights.

Back then, the Templars' ride outs were more for marauding, whereas ours were about celebrating our ancestry and our love of traversing the desert into the mountains of Paso Robles on horseback.

I couldn't help but wish Uncle Tryst was here. I missed him in the same way I did my father. Both men had been my mentors. Tryst still was; I just didn't see him as often as I wanted.

When my dad passed away, Tryst had taken over the role of most senior member of the secret society. Four years ago, he'd stepped aside to care for my aunt, and since I was next in age, it was now up to me to call the meeting to order.

Along with Ridge and me, three of my blood brothers—Enzo, better known as Cru, Snapper, and Kick—were seated at the table. Press, Beau, and Zin were also here.

I cleared my throat. "As you're all aware, the Olallieberry Diner was destroyed by fire."

Press raised a hand. "I thought it might be easier if I compiled a dossier to bring everyone up to speed on what we know thus far."

I thanked him as he passed copies around the table. I sat and read through mine, allowing the others to do the same.

"There's been a new development I haven't had a chance to brief Press on," I began. "Earlier today, Vader shared a photo with me of a message written in the ashes on the diner's concrete foundation. It said, 'Pay up or the house is next.' The sheriff has two deputies currently surveilling Peg's place. I brought her and Addison here to the ranch for the time being."

"Any update on Murphy's whereabouts?" Zin asked.

"Negative," responded Snapper. "At least not through our channels."

I looked around the table, but no one else spoke.

"I have a proposal."

"Go ahead, Brix," said Ridge.

"As you read in Press' report, we believe Murphy is indebted to the Killeen Organization. Here is what I propose. First, we go directly to the top and initiate contact with James Dunn. I am prepared to offer to pay off the gambling debt, then take it a step further."

I looked around the room and saw no sign of disagreement so far.

"I will offer an additional sum, to be agreed upon today, in exchange for the Killeens delivering Murphy to us."

"Dead or alive?" asked Cru.

"Preferably alive."

"That will be harder for them to guarantee."

"We'll accept dead," said Ridge, leaning forward and resting his elbows on the table. "Cleaner that way, Brix. Plus, if you believe the Killeens are responsible for the fire, they will be less likely to agree to your terms if you insist on his being delivered alive." He looked around the room. "Who will make contact?"

"I will," said Zin before I could respond.

"I'm in too," added Press. I wasn't surprised about either offer. We all considered Zin our personal attorney as well as that of the Caballeros. And in the same way I was closer to Ridge than the others at the table, Press and Zin were too.

"Next, we need to determine the amount of the bounty."

Ridge sat back in his seat. "Before we get to that, Brix, I want to clarify funding."

"Of course. I'll provide whatever is needed."

"Are all in agreement?" my best friend asked.

Cru pushed his chair back and stood. "I'm not."

This was a blow I hadn't anticipated. Why wouldn't my brother be in agreement? My eyes met his.

"You aren't funding this alone, Brix. Peg and Addy are important to all of us."

"I appreciate it, but—"

"Show of hands," said Ridge. "Who's in?" Everyone at the table raised their arm. "Now that we've cleared up the consensus on funding, proceed with determining the amount."

After much discussion, we all decided that going to the Killeens with anything but our best offer would make us look weak. The other thing we agreed on was that getting Dennis Murphy out of Peg and Addison's lives was worth going in strong.

"We double the payoff, so the bounty is equal to the debt," Ridge suggested.

It was the amount I'd initially planned to offer and was glad that, again, no hesitation was expressed, let alone disagreement.

No one left when I adjourned the meeting. While I wanted to touch base with each man individually, the first I needed to talk to was Cru.

"How are things with the crush?" I asked, joining him on the other side of the room. My fear in asking was that the Butler brothers had taken over, leaving Cru essentially in the same position he'd been in with me.

"We're close. I'm holding off on the eastside vineyards. I'd like to increase our production of late-harvest Zinfandel, and pushing when we pick can get us where we want to be sugar-wise and with Brix."

My father had given me the nickname when I was a teenager and became obsessed with the measurement as well as the tool—a refractometer—we used to calculate "degrees Brix."

Essentially, the tool was used to evaluate the refraction of light passing through a liquid sample—as little as the juice from one grape. Since liquids containing sugar were denser than water, they caused greater refraction as light passed through.

Why did we need to know degrees Brix? Because it helped us determine when to pick, based on the approximate alcohol level of the wine we made from particular vineyards.

While the story my father told regarding my nickname related to my obsession with the refractometer, my true passion at that age was more about pushing alcohol content.

"Has Naughton weighed in on this plan?"

Cru's jaw dropped, and I realized I'd worded my question wrong. When I put my hand on his arm, he moved it away from me.

"I don't give a shit about Naughton Butler's opinion," my brother spat.

"Neither do I."

"What?"

"I'm sorry, Cru. What I really wanted to know was whether this was his idea or yours."

"Like I said, what Naughton thinks—"

"Doesn't matter to me, either, Enzo. What I'm trying to say, and doing a crappy job of, is that I trust whatever decisions you make and consider those to be final."

He studied me. "Since when?"

I wanted to say always, but we both knew that was bullshit. Up until this crush, I would've second-guessed whatever my brother came to me with. Not that there would've been much; that was on me too.

"I'm handing off more of the main label to you, effective immediately."

He was completely justified in his evident skepticism. "Which varietals?"

"I'd like to sit down and talk it over, but for now, I'm going to need you to oversee all production until further notice."

Cru's expression softened. "Is there something you aren't telling me?"

Stepping away for just a couple of days gave me a better perspective of my life. If I continued the way I had been, I would end up like my father—gone from this world far too young. In his case, though, he'd married the love of his life and raised a family with her. The only thing I'd accomplished was to make wine, and even that, he'd handed down to me.

"Time to reassess my life," I said when I realized I hadn't responded. "My priorities are fucked up."

Cru smiled. "You are fucked up. I'll give you that." He put his hand on my shoulder. "Whatever I can do to help. I mean that sincerely, Brix."

"I was telling Addison how much I missed walking the vineyards with Pop. She asked why I didn't walk them with you, and I realized I'd never asked you to join me."

"I could have offered as easily." Cru put his hands on the back of a chair. "When would you like to meet?"

"Would as soon as we're finished here work?"

Cru smiled. "Whenever, boss."

I laughed and walked away from my brother when Ridge caught my eye.

"Everything okay?" he asked when I approached.

"No, but it's nothing new with Cru."

My friend was familiar with my struggles with my sibling and nodded. "You said Addy and her mom are here?"

"Yes, at the main house. Although my mother is pushing Addison to stay with me."

Ridge laughed. "Your mother is? Not you?"

If I tried to explain that I wanted to wait to have sex with Addison until after the bachelor auction, would he even believe me? I still hadn't told him I'd agreed to be in it. "She has a lot going on in her life," I said instead. "I also figured Peg would be more comfortable if her daughter was with her."

"Interesting," he mumbled.

"I know you're telling yourself this is due to the lecture you gave me, but it was a decision I made long before that."

"I'm not following. You made the decision that Addy should stay at Los Cab with your mom and hers long *before* we talked several hours ago?"

Well, shit. I'd commented based on my real reason for Addison to stay with my mom rather than what I'd just told him. "I don't want to rush her."

He nodded slowly. "Got it."

"Shut the fuck up," I muttered.

Ridge raised both hands. "I didn't say anything other than that I understood. For the record, *when* you made that decision doesn't matter, Brix. I'm just proud of you for making it at all."

He was proud of me? I rolled my eyes and changed the subject. "Sure wish Tryst was here."

"Actually, what I'd prefer is to be at his ranch."

"You and me both."

My uncle had owned his five-thousand-acre ranch in Mexico for several years before he built on it. He'd started with a temple followed by the water room. It was similar to a pump house, but like every other structure on the property, it was designed and constructed using the traditional Indian architectural system known as *Vastu shastra.*

Vastu itself was the science of keeping the five elements of nature—earth, water, fire, air, and space—in balance. When it was applied to building design, the idea was to maximize "positive vibrational energy" in order to create a space that was a spiritual and healing sanctuary.

While I may have inwardly scoffed at the notion when Tryst had initially explained it to me, as soon as I entered the ranch's primary dwelling, a sense of peace washed over me. It wasn't something I'd admitted to anyone outside of my brothers and the rest of our close group of friends—all of whom confessed a similar experience when they paid their own visit.

Now, in addition to the first two structures and the main house, there was a meditation building and several guest *casitas*—all of which were designed in the Vastu system.

In every case, the center space was empty and the surrounding rooms were situated based on the most "auspicious" of the cardinal directions—north, south, east, and west—along with the four intercardinal directions—northwest, northeast, southwest, and southeast. I didn't really understand why, but as an example, Tryst had informed me that one would *never* have a kitchen positioned in the northeast part of a house.

Whether I believed any of this made a difference in how a structure was built, didn't change how I felt when I was there.

Even before he knew his wife was ill, my uncle had named the ranch *El Lugar de Curación*, or the Healing Place. While my beloved aunt Rosa's cancer hadn't been cured by living there, the final years of her life were as peaceful and tranquil as my uncle could possibly have made them.

Ridge's reminder of the ranch made me want to share it with Addison as much or more as her tree house. I innately knew it was a place she'd appreciate.

"You're thinking about taking her there, aren't you?"

"Sorry. What?"

Ridge smirked. "Addy. You're thinking of taking her to the ranch."

"Don't strain a muscle, patting yourself on the back. It wouldn't take a genius to come to that conclusion."

14

Addison

The amount of things Brix had to catch up on would likely take several hours, rather than the couple he'd predicted, but after spending so much time together, I missed him.

He'd stunned me when he said he came to Stave just to see me. While it wasn't easy to admit, at the beginning of my shifts, I'd find myself hoping he'd come in at some point. On the nights he left after a single glass of wine, I was always disappointed he hadn't stayed longer.

"I'm so glad you and my Gabe are finally together," said his mother, coming to stand next to me by the kitchen window.

"I'm not sure we're together, Mrs. Avila. We're—"

"Call me Lucia, and of course you're together. I always knew you would be. I was just afraid it would take too many years for you both to realize it."

"Mrs., err, Lucia, Brix is helping my mom and me, and while I appreciate it, I wouldn't read too much into it."

She patted my hand. "And that is why you're standing at the window, watching for him to return."

I shrugged. "If you think my mom will be okay, I'm going to take a walk."

"She's napping, so this would be the perfect time for you to go."

"I have to remember to take her back to the hospital so they can put a cast on her arm," I said more to myself than her, biting my lip.

"*Mija*, don't punish yourself for not knowing. Women in relationships like your mother had with her husband work very hard to hide the abuse."

"I heard them argue." Why hadn't I ever intervened? Even if it hadn't escalated into physical abuse, wasn't verbal just as bad?

When Brix's mother pulled me into a hug, I couldn't stop myself from crying. I hated that it seemed I was feeling sorry for myself when it was my mother I pitied.

"Here is Gabe now," she said, pulling back and pointing to the truck barreling toward the house. "I'd say he missed you as much as you missed him."

I couldn't help but smile at her assumptions about the nature of the relationship between her son and me. Nor could I stop myself from wishing it really was the way she saw it, especially when he pulled up near the porch and climbed out of the cab. The sight of him always left me breathless. While all the Avila brothers were handsome in their own way, Brix was the only one that made my heart pound.

He caught me watching from the window, smiled, and waved.

"Go on now," said Lucia, opening the back door and pushing me through it.

"Hi," I said, putting my hands on Brix's chest when he raced up the steps and pulled me into his arms.

"Hi," he replied before bringing his lips to mine in a kiss that felt hot enough to scorch the earth. Before my brain drained of a single thought other than how his tongue felt when it pushed into my mouth, I couldn't help but wonder if his mother was watching.

"I was on my way to the winery but couldn't drive by the house without stopping in to kiss you."

"Oh." I spoke before there was time for me to mask my disappointment.

"Did you miss me?"

The way he stared into my eyes, I couldn't lie. "I did."

Brix tightened his hold around my waist and rested the side of his face against my hair. "Thank you for admitting it, Addison. I worry about how overwhelming it must be with my sudden inability to keep my hands off you." He pulled away again to look into my eyes.

"If you're waiting for me to admit it, yes, I am a bit overwhelmed." I felt my cheeks flush. "Not that I want you to stop."

"Come with me. I'll try to make it quick."

"It's okay, Brix. Go do what you need to do. I'll be fine."

He smiled; it was so beautiful, and I loved seeing it as often as I was lately. "I won't be fine. I don't like being away from you, baby."

Could I admit I didn't like being away from him either? Soon, though, we'd have to be. Once everything with Dennis was sorted, Brix and I would go back to our own busy lives. Hopefully, he'd still come to Stave to see me.

"Speaking of being away from you, have you given any more thought to where you want to stay?"

I shook my head. "I want to talk to my mom first. Alone."

"Good luck with that," he said, laughing.

"Which is why I think you should go to the winery by yourself."

He stuck out his lower lip. "I guess I can't argue with you needing to talk to your mom." He brushed my lips with his. "Can we plan on dinner at least? Alone?"

I looked over and caught Lucia peeking out the window at us and smirked. "Good luck with that."

After walking away and turning around to kiss me four more times, leaving me in giggles, Brix finally climbed into his truck and drove off.

I wasn't lying when I said I didn't want him to stop overwhelming me. I'd never experienced this kind of attention from a man and certainly never had a boyfriend as "into me" as Brix seemed to be. It was hard to tamp down the feelings of insecurity I'd lived with most of my life, mainly based on my appearance. But with every kiss he gave me, they lessened.

That he and I might have sex if I stayed with him instead of at his mom's house was so intimidating that I almost hoped my mom begged me to stay with her.

"Hey, Mom," I said when she came out of the kitchen door.

She motioned to two chairs on the porch. "Sit with me, Addy?"

"Of course."

Several minutes passed without her saying anything. I was about to start when I heard her voice catch.

"I…I want you to know how sorry I am."

"You have nothing to be sorry for."

"I do, Addy." She closed her eyes and turned her face toward the sun. "There are things I should've told you."

"You were scared. I get that."

"I was ashamed. I still am."

"You shouldn't feel that way with your own daughter."

"Especially with you."

"Look, soon this will be over and you can get on with the rest of your life. Have you thought about what you'll do once you get the money from the insurance?"

My mom stared out at the horizon, then shook her head as though she'd come out of a fog. "The diner has been part of this community for years. The fact that it's gone because of me breaks my heart. I can't afford to rebuild, though."

"It isn't gone because of you. It's gone because of Dennis. While people will miss it, I'm sure there isn't a single person in Cambria—or the surrounding area—who won't understand that you can't rebuild."

"I just hope it's enough money to pay off the bank." She bit her bottom lip in the same way I did when I was worried about something. "And I pray that Conrad is right about whoever Dennis owes money to not burning down the house too." Her eyes filled with tears. "I don't think I could take it."

I understood. It was hard to imagine that things *could* get worse, but the message left certainly indicated the possibility. It made my eyes fill with tears too.

My mom reached over and took my hand in hers. "I'm sorry, Addy," she repeated.

"I know you are, Mom."

"Brix is a good man," she said after a few minutes of neither of us talking.

"He is," I agreed. Two words—whether it was my agreement or her saying he was a "good man"—didn't scratch the surface of the truth of it. I couldn't imagine anyone stepping up to help us in the way he had. It was sad to say, but I couldn't think of many others who would have to the same extent.

"I'll be fine with Lucia, Addy. You don't need to stay here because you're worried about me."

"What if I don't want to stay with Brix?" I winked.

"Then, I'd say you're crazy." We both laughed, and it felt so good.

"I don't know, Mom. It's moving kinda fast."

She raised a brow. "I know he stayed at the apartment with you."

I almost bit my lower lip, but stopped myself. "Nothing happened."

"Just because you're a guest in his house doesn't mean anything has to happen."

While she may be right, she obviously hadn't witnessed some of our kisses. I was more worried about our being able to keep our hands off each other.

"If you have a chance at happiness, don't turn your back on it, sweetheart. Take it from me."

"Is that what you did?"

She shrugged her shoulder and shook her head. "I don't know. Your father…"

I stood. This wasn't a conversation I wanted to have right now. Maybe not ever, but especially right now. Neither of us needed to think about things that would make us more unhappy.

"I was considering a walk. Do you want to join me?"

"I'll stay here if you don't mind."

I told her I didn't, pulled my jacket tighter, and walked down the porch steps. I really didn't know where I was going, but I had a decent sense of direction, so I didn't worry about getting lost.

Fifteen minutes later, when I came out of a forested area and stepped into a clearing, I was surprised to find myself near the rear entrance of the winery.

Before I could turn around and go in the opposite direction, Brix walked out of a side door followed by Cru. I took a few steps back, leaned up against a tree, and watched him.

He looked more like the Brix I was used to seeing. Between his scowl and his hands on his hips, I sensed the two men disagreed about the topic of their conversation. When he reached out and slammed his fist into the stone side of the building, I knew it was far worse than a disagreement.

Something else I now knew was that Brix had the kind of temper that made him hit things when he was angry. One I'd never witnessed in him before. Seeing it made me sick to my stomach.

15
Brix

"I'm sorry, man," said my brother as I shook my head at the same time I shook the hand I'd just bloodied.

Zin's call to say he and Press had already made contact with the Killeens had stunned me, but their response to our offer was what made me lose my temper in a way I hadn't before in my life.

"They just declined? No explanation? No counteroffer?" asked Cru.

"That's what Zin said."

"Now what?"

I gazed out at our property, hating how out of control I felt. I thought I saw something—someone—out of the corner of my eye, but when I turned my head, either I'd been imagining things or they were gone.

"Have Trev check the security feeds."

Cru nodded and pulled out his phone.

While it was nearly impossible for someone to gain access to the ranch without our granting it, there had been times when the security systems went down. Rather than risk anyone's safety, we'd check.

"He's ten-seven," said Cru, studying his phone in the same way I studied him. The code meant "out of communication," which was impossible. We could *always* reach Trev on the number I knew my brother had called. That particular phone was used solely for emergencies.

In the event Trev had to step away for any length of time—even to use the restroom—he knew to hit the single button that would forward any call coming in on that line to Cru, Snapper, Kick, me, and the rest of the Caballeros. When that didn't happen, my hackles raised.

"What's his twenty?"

Cru opened the app that would tell us where every member of our family was, even Alex, her husband, and their daughter.

"The caves."

"Which part?"

"Right inside the main entrance."

Worry ate at my stomach. "Find Snapper and Kick. Tell one to meet me there and the other to meet you at the house."

"On it," said Cru, taking off in the direction of his vehicle without my needing to explain that I wanted him to ensure Addison, her mother, and our mother were safe.

As I rounded the corner and jumped into my truck, I called Ridge. "Trev's gone dark."

"Shit," he muttered. "Where do you want me?"

"Back here as soon as you can. He pinged at the caves. That's where I'm headed now."

"On my way."

"Cru is going to the house. Get everyone else back here too."

"Roger that."

I stepped on the gas and raced toward the caves, knowing that as much as I wanted to go straight to the house myself, I'd asked Cru to go instead for a reason. I couldn't send him into the danger I feared our brother was in. *I* had to be the one to locate Trev.

A feeling of impending doom settled over me when I pulled up near the side of the entrance and didn't see my brother's truck. The gate I remembered locking behind me after everyone left the meeting earlier, was wide open.

I pulled my gun out of the console safe after unlocking it, and got out, keeping close to the rocks as I eased toward the gate now creaking as it swung in the breeze.

Creeping around the corner, I held my gun at the ready. Based on the locator I'd looked at a few minutes ago, he shouldn't be far. I remained as silent as possible, listening for any indication Trev or anyone else was close by.

As I turned to the left and into the first tasting room, I saw him.

"Trev!" I called, racing forward to where he was on the floor, his arms and legs bound, blood pooling near his head. I checked for a pulse with one hand while keeping my gun pointed in the direction of the doorway with the other. When I detected a heartbeat and signs of breathing, I set down my weapon and removed my shirt.

"Jesus!" shouted Kick, running over to where I knelt, trying to stop the flow of blood from my brother's head.

"He's out but still with us," I told him as I listened to him call for help. "Naughton, this is Kick Avila. We need medical transport. My brother Trev is down. Entrance to the caves."

Both Naught and Maddox had their pilot's license and were able to fly the helicopter they kept on a pad at Butler Ranch, virtually next door.

It seemed seconds later when I heard the blades start up and it lift off. What seemed longer were the minutes that ticked by without my brother regaining consciousness.

"I'll go meet him," said Kick as I carefully looked for signs of further injury and cut Trev's bindings loose.

"What happened to him?" asked Naughton when he and Kick raced in with the stretcher.

"All I can find is a head wound, but he was restrained."

"Copy that," said Naughton, getting into position and counting to three before the three of us moved my brother from the floor to the stretcher.

"I'll go with him. You're needed here," said Kick. Before I could ask what else had happened, my cell rang.

"Brix," I answered without looking to see who was calling.

"Mom is here. Banged up, but fine, but Brix—Addy and Peg are gone." I could hardly hear Cru's words above the blood pounding in my ears. My eyes met Kick's as I raced in front of them and to my truck.

"Take care of Trev," I shouted behind me.

I didn't bother with roads; I went across fields, the fastest way I knew to where Addison was supposed to be. As I drove, I wouldn't allow myself to think about what may have happened or who was responsible for the way I'd found Trevino.

Ridge was waiting for me when I pulled up as close to the house as I could get.

"Lucia said two men, masked and dressed in black, burst through the door. One tied her up while the other did the same to Peg. One of them pistol-whipped your mom, and when she came to, Cru was here but Peg was gone."

"What about Addison?"

"Your mom said she wasn't here. She'd gone for a walk."

Which meant there was a chance whoever had Peg had her too; there was an equal chance they didn't. "How long ago?" I asked as he followed me up the steps and into the house.

"She isn't sure."

"Oh, *mijo*," my mother cried, holding her hand out to me. *"¡Estaba tan asustada!"*

"I'm sure you were terrified, Mama. Can you tell me everything you remember?"

When she finished her recollection, I didn't know more than Ridge had already told me.

"Brix?" he said, motioning me over to where he stood in the kitchen and out of earshot of my mother. "Trev is in the ER and stable. He came to and told a similar story to Lucia's. He was double-checking the gate into the caves because he received an alert it was open. Two men, masked and all in black, jumped him."

"I locked it. I'm sure of it."

"Press went and took a look. There are signs of tampering."

"Murphy wouldn't have this kind of manpower. It's gotta be the Killeens."

"My first thought too, but why?"

"It doesn't make any sense," I said at the same time I saw Zin pull up and jump out of his car. I wondered if he'd have the answer to Ridge's question.

"Hey," he said, rubbing the back of his neck as he walked up the porch steps to meet us.

"I just told Ridge this has to be the work of the Killeens, but why?"

He shook his head. "It isn't."

My eyes opened wide. "Who, then?"

"FAIM."

"*That's* who Murphy owes the money to?"

"Negative. That's who's backing him."

"Fuck," Ridge and I muttered at almost the same time.

The so-called Family Affiliated Irish Mafia was nothing more than a street gang born out of west Contra Costa County rather than Cork or County Clare. Their ties to anything Irish were dubious, and they certainly had none to the actual Irish Mafia.

That they operated one of the largest crystal methamphetamine distribution networks in the world made them more notorious and deadlier than the Killeens, who were bigger into racketeering. If FAIM was backing Murphy, he'd have plenty of manpower—from scumbags just like him.

I couldn't see any logical reason for them jumping Trev other than to create a distraction, which meant they knew far too much about Los Cab's security systems, and I said so.

"Press and Beau are running through security footage. They also made contact with Burns," Ridge responded.

Burns Butler was my sister's father-in-law. To her, he was Coco's kindly Grandpa Laird. To those in the intelligence world, which Los Cab operated on the periphery of, he was the world's leading expert on security.

"Murphy's affiliation with FAIM is the reason the Killeens turned down our offer," said Ridge.

Zin nodded. "My assumption as well."

None of that mattered at the moment. Peg was missing, and for all intents, so was Addison. It didn't matter who took one or both of them; only finding them did.

I pulled out my phone, wishing I'd thought to track hers.

"We need to mobilize," I heard Ridge say, putting voice to my own thoughts. While I couldn't stand around doing nothing, I had no idea where to start. It was like my brain was in a fog. My decision-making ability—something I rarely, if ever, struggled with—was thwarted.

"Where is everyone?" I asked.

"On their way to the caves," answered Ridge, looking at his phone. "If you're comfortable leaving your mom here alone, we should head there too."

"What's going on?" asked Alex, bursting in through the back door with Maddox right behind her. "Mad got a message from Laird, saying we should get here ASAP."

When my eyes met Ridge's, he ran through everything we knew and what we didn't. "Can the two of you stay with Lucia?" he asked.

Alex put her hand on my arm. "You find our girl and Peg," she said with tears in her eyes. "Mad and I will take care of Mom."

"We've got this," Maddox added when my sister left the room. "Go."

"Has anyone contacted Vader?" Ridge asked when we reached the parked vehicles.

"I'll do that now," Zin said before closing his door at the same time I got in the passenger side of Ridge's truck.

"Go that way," I pointed when Ridge backed up and before he could veer in the direction of the road. He nodded and followed the tracks left by my truck, going in the opposite direction.

My eyes met Zin's when he got out of his car and walked to the cave's entrance. "He had an emergency call. Said he'll get right back to me."

"Were you able to inform him of Peg's and Addy's disappearances?" Ridge asked.

"Affirmative. The call came in before he had a chance to respond."

When my cell rang a few seconds later, I jolted in hopeful surprise. I unlocked the screen, praying it would be Addison. When I saw it was Vader calling, my heart sank.

"Yeah?" I said, accepting the call and putting it directly on speaker.

"Brix, I need you and Zin to meet me at the station as soon as you can. There's been a development."

"What?"

"We'll talk when you get here." The solemnity of his words hit hard. If either were injured, he certainly wouldn't be asking me to meet him at the station. However, his tone conveyed something was seriously wrong.

"Fuck, Vader. Don't pull this bullshit. If you know, tell me Addison and Peg are okay."

"Just get to the station, Brix."

"What's going on?" Ridge asked.

"I'm not sure, other than Vader summoned Zin and me. Something tells me we're going to need Tryst's help."

"He's already on his way." Ridge looked at his phone. "Should arrive within the hour."

"Come on, Brix. I'll drive," said Zin.

16

Brix

I almost wept in relief when I walked in and could see Addison and her mother through the window of the conference room—until I took a good look at Peg.

I was about to open the door and ask what the hell had happened when Vader put his hand on the knob. "I can't let you go in there."

"Why not?"

He motioned with his head. "Come into my office."

"Hold up," said Zin. "Why is there a deputy in with them?"

"Like I said, come with me."

Zin shook his head. "You have a law enforcement officer in a room with my clients. I'm not going anywhere until I speak with them."

Vader let out a heavy sigh. "The deputy knows better than to question either woman, Zin. Just come with me, and I'll explain."

"The sooner we get this out of the way, the sooner we can both talk to them," I said, putting my hand on my friend's arm. "Right now, I just want to know what the fuck is going on."

Vader closed the door of his office and told us to take a seat. I would've argued, but the man's body language told me there was something serious he needed to discuss with us.

"Dennis Murphy is dead. I've got forensics and two of my men processing the scene."

This wasn't bad news as far as I was concerned, but obviously, Vader thought it was. *"And?"*

He rested his forearms on his desk. "The neighbor called it in to me directly. When we arrived at the house, Addy confessed to killing him."

"You took her confession?" barked Zin.

The sheriff glared at him. "She blurted it out without any prompting from me, and I was the one who stopped her from saying anything else."

I held up my hand. "Hang on. The house?"

"Her mother's house."

"So they had them both?"

"Given I wouldn't allow either woman to tell me any more than Addy already did, I have no idea what led up to the murder."

"Murder? This was self-defense, right?"

Vader shook his head. "He was unarmed."

How could he have held both Addison and Peg if he was unarmed? "He might not have had a weapon, but we both know he was capable of killing without one."

"Like I said, I stopped Addy from saying another word, but, Brix, after just a peripheral look at the crime scene, something doesn't add up."

Zin stood. "I want to talk to my client, Sheriff. *Now.*"

Vader looked at him, but I held my hand up a second time.

"Look, we both know you shouldn't have called us down here, and you shouldn't be telling us the things you are. Thank you, Vader."

"You're welcome," he said to me before glaring at Zin. "I had the deputy stay in the room with strict instructions that if either woman said a word, he was to notify me immediately. It's my recommendation that we separate them, but that's your call, Counselor."

We both waited for Zin to respond.

"It's a good idea," he conceded without looking at either Vader or me.

"Who do you want to talk to first?"

"Addy."

Vader nodded and stood. "You wait here," he said to me, pointing at the chair I'd just gotten out of.

"No."

"Yes, Brix," said Zin. "I need to talk to her alone first." He looked at the sheriff. "Is her confession on the record?"

"It is."

"When can she be arraigned?"

"If we do it here, tomorrow morning at the earliest."

"Can you hold her here overnight?" Zin asked.

"I can make an exception."

The Cambria police station had a single jail cell that was only meant to hold someone a few hours before they could be transferred to the county jail in San Luis Obispo.

"Appreciate it, Vader." Zin looked from him to me. "I'll make it as quick as I can, Brix."

While I'd acquiesced and stayed in Vader's office. I couldn't sit. Instead, I paced the small quarters. The minutes ticking by felt like hours. I had no idea where the sheriff had gone or why it was taking Zin so long to talk with Addy. Clearly, this was self-defense.

There could be no question. Dennis Murphy had not only physically abused his wife, he'd also attempted to take her life in order to cash in on a million-dollar life insurance policy. It was cut and dry as far as I was concerned.

All I cared about now was holding Addison in my arms and never letting go again.

When Zin returned to Vader's office, I went straight for the door. He pushed me out of the way and stood so I couldn't get past him. "Hang on, Brix."

"No! I've waited long enough. I need to see her. Get out of my fucking way, Zin."

"She doesn't want to see you."

"What? That's crazy. *Move!*"

Zin put both his hands on my shoulders. "Listen carefully. She…doesn't…want…to…see…you."

I took a step back, trying to process my friend's words. I felt like I'd been hit hard in the gut.

"What happened to your hand?"

I held it up. "I punched a wall. Why?"

"You tell me."

"What do you mean?"

"Why'd you punch the wall, Brix?"

"It was right after you called and told me the Killeens wouldn't accept our offer."

"Where were you?"

"At the winery with Cru. What the fuck, Zin? Why are you asking me all these questions, and what does it have to do with Addison not wanting to see me?"

"Because she *did* see you. She saw you do it."

I stared at the bruises on my hand, then up at Zin. "How?"

"She was there."

My mind reeled with how that could've been possible. "It was her I saw in the woods," I muttered.

"Makes sense."

"I need to explain." I got that seeing me react in anger the way I had would've freaked her out, but not that she wouldn't give me a chance to tell her why I had. "It isn't like her, Zin."

"I think there's more to it. She's sticking to her story about being the one who killed Murphy, but I don't think she pulled the trigger."

"She's protecting Peg."

"Probably, but there isn't much I can do to get her to recant. Not that it would make a difference. Barring coercion, there aren't a lot of ways for me to get her confession thrown out without hard evidence someone else did it or that she couldn't have."

"I *need* to see her. Make it happen."

"I can't."

My arm itched to hit the nearest wall. Either that or Zin, but me reacting that way was the reason Addison was refusing to see me. "You think she's using that as an excuse not to talk to me because she's afraid I'll know she's lying."

"That or something like it."

"What about Peg?"

"I haven't talked to her yet. Given Addison's intransigence, I think it would be best if someone else represents her mother."

"Good idea. Who?"

"Let me make a couple of calls, and I'll get back to you on that. For now, Vader has promised to keep Addy here overnight rather than have her moved to the county lockup. He's also made arrangements to have Judge Sorenson meet us here first thing tomorrow morning to arraign her."

I knew most of this from the conversation the two men had before they left the office.

"He could get himself in hot water for this, Brix."

"No shit. Where is he now?"

"With Peg. Another thing he shouldn't be doing, but there's no way to talk him out of it."

"Meaning what?"

"Just hope no one sees her going in or out of Vader's house."

"I don't know what to do. I can't just leave Addison here."

"You don't have a choice. In terms of what you need to do, I think that would be obvious."

"Gather the troops?"

"Damn straight. If Addy won't save herself, we'll have to do it for her."

By the time we got to the caves and through the secret corridor to the meeting room, everyone else had arrived, including my uncle. I approached and he stood. "Thank you for coming."

"Of course. Ridge said it was imperative. Why are we here, Brix?"

I motioned for everyone to take a seat. "One of our own is in trouble."

"Who?" Tryst asked, looking around the room. "All nine of us are here."

I dipped my chin in acknowledgment. "Fair enough." I steepled my fingers on the large table in front of me. "It's Addison Reagan."

Cru, Snapper, and Kick looked at me with wide eyes. "What happened?" asked the latter.

"She's been arrested," Ridge answered, saving me from revealing the emotion the words would evoke.

I swallowed and finished the sentence. "For murder."

The only people in the room who didn't appear in a state of shock were Zin, Ridge, and me, and only because I'd called Ridge on our way here to brief him on what had happened. I'd also asked him not to say anything until we arrived.

"She confessed to shooting Dennis Murphy and is being held at the Cambria police station until her arraignment tomorrow. Before you ask, Vader is keeping her there against protocol," said Zin.

"Is Murphy the one who abducted Addy and her mother?" Cru asked.

"I don't have a definitive answer to that question yet," Zin responded.

I'd been so focused on Addison—first her arrest and then that she wouldn't see me—I hadn't thought to ask Vader about the abduction.

"You said Addy confessed?" asked Tryst, leaning forward and steepling his hands like mine were.

"Vader stopped her from saying more than she had, but yes, she confessed," I answered.

Tryst's eyes bored into mine. "Do you believe she did it?"

"Not for a minute."

"She's protecting someone."

"Her mother." The answer was easy. What to do about it was not.

"My intention is to have her plead not guilty tomorrow morning and request bail. Given the judge is local and knows Addy and Peg, as well as their financial circumstances and about the fire that destroyed the diner, I anticipate he'll grant it."

"Whatever the bond is, I'll post it," I told him.

Zin nodded in a way that indicated he'd expected I would. "Once we get Addy released, there's the question of her mother's and her safety. We still don't know the details of the abduction or the extent of Murphy's affiliation with FAIM. Primarily, whether there will be retaliation for his death. There's also the issue of the money he owed the Killeens. While they didn't want to play ball and accept our offer of a bounty, they aren't going to walk away from a couple hundred thousand bucks."

I was willing to pay off the man's debts too, but that wasn't something that needed to be discussed now. Offering to do so may result in them blackmailing me to keep the money coming.

"We've made sure the security at Los Cab is airtight," said Snapper.

"I question whether Addy or her mother would be comfortable coming back here," said Zin. I appreciated the way he'd worded the statement rather than telling them the woman who'd crawled into my heart didn't want to see me.

"Let's circle back to her confession," continued Tryst. "From the brief I read after your last meeting—my apologies for not getting here sooner—there was evidence Murphy physically abused Addy's mother. If he was the one who abducted the two women, there should be no question this was done in self-defense."

"According to Vader, Murphy was unarmed. I'll know more tomorrow, once I can take a look at what they processed at the crime scene," Zin responded.

I watched the exchange, never more thankful that he was both an attorney and the kind of friend who answered my uncle's questions innately, knowing I wasn't in the right frame of mind to do so myself.

I checked the time on my phone, hating that Addison would be in that jail all alone tonight. Every part of me was pulled to drive right there, force my way in, and insist Addison talk to me. Only my respect for her request not to see me stopped me from bulldozing my way into the station. If I'd somehow managed to convince either Zin or Vader to allow me to before we left earlier, she would've been trapped. Forced to talk to me against her will. I never wanted her to feel that way.

"Excuse me," I said, standing and walking out of the room. Rather than text Vader, I called him. "Who's with her?"

"Brix?"

"You know it's me. Who is with Addison?"

"Deputy Sanchez."

I was glad a woman was with her, instead of one of the men. "Vader, tell Sanchez she should call me if Addison is scared or needs anything or, you know, anything."

His voice softened. "I will."

"Swear it."

"Hang on." I heard shuffling, then a door opening and closing. "I have Addy's mother here with me, Brix.

Believe me, if you don't think I'm checking in with Elizabeth once an hour, you aren't thinking straight."

"Just promise either you or Sanchez will call me if Addison needs *anything*."

"I promise. Now, get some sleep."

I would be doing nothing of the kind, and I assumed Vader knew that. I doubted he'd be getting any either.

Before I could return to the meeting room, Zin came out. "I'll be in touch in the morning," he said before exiting the caves.

Tryst was right behind him. "I want to talk with you alone for a moment if you'll indulge me."

"Of course. What can I do for you, Uncle?"

"It's what I'm prepared to do for you."

"Go on."

"I will be posting Addy's bail tomorrow."

"That isn't necessary."

"You're right. It's imperative."

I studied him, realizing in that instant what he was really proposing. "Tryst—"

"Until we can figure out a way for Addy to recant her confession while, at the same time, protecting Peg, we have no choice, Brix."

"Even if we do what I know you're suggesting, I can't allow you to be the one to post her bail."

"You must, Gabriel. Otherwise, you risk Los Caballeros."

"And you risk *your* ranch."

"She will return long before that happens."

"Then, it isn't any different for me."

"The decision has been made, and it is final."

I turned my head in the direction of the room we were about to reenter and saw by his expression that Ridge had heard every word.

Before I could speak, he did.

"I'm in agreement, Brix. We all are—except Zin. As an officer of the court, he cannot know what we have planned or share his opinion."

"How will this work if she continues to refuse to see me?"

"Tryst and I will handle it," said Ridge.

I shook my head. If Addison was being transported out of the country, there was no way in hell I wasn't going with her.

17

Brix

"I don't want to veer off subject, but Kick and I think we know who sabotaged the security system," said Snapper when Ridge, Tryst, and I returned to the room. "We reviewed the backup footage Burns showed us how to access."

"Can you identify the person?"

Kick sneered. "I can. It was Connor Reilly."

Cru stood up so fast the chair he'd been sitting in toppled to the floor. "That fucking *sonuvabitch*," he spat.

Connor had worked directly for Cru and was fired when Kick found him in the winery office, a place where he had no business being. While that may or may not have been grounds for firing him, when Kick questioned him, the man told him to fuck off and then got violent. That led to him losing his job.

"Fucking meth head," I heard my youngest brother mutter.

"Find the asshole," I seethed. "You know what to do with him when you do."

"We'll help," offered Press, pointing at himself, then at his brother.

"I'll let the five of you formulate your own plan. Let me know when you've got him here, and I'll join you."

I caught a look pass between Press, Ridge, and my uncle, but didn't care enough at the moment to question it. I had too much on my mind.

Certain things were falling into place for me in terms of what may have happened when Trev was attacked and Peg and Addison were taken from the ranch. When Kick said Reilly was a meth head, it made me think the man would likely have ties to FAIM as well as to Murphy—if he was really being backed by them.

Likely Murphy got the gang of thugs to protect him by offering them money. Given the amount he owed the Killeens in gambling debts, the only way he could get his hands on enough cash to pay them back was with Peg's life insurance policy. In order for that to happen, she had to be dead.

It was easy to imagine Murphy offering a few of his FAIM buddies a share of the payout to get them to not only kidnap Peg and Addison, but kill them too. As

Kick said, Reilly himself was a meth head. If my theory proved correct, the rest of the thugs who had attacked Trev and kidnapped the women likely were too.

It also wouldn't have taken much for them to agree to help. Maybe as little as ten or twenty-five grand each—which would cover the cost of enough meth hits to ensure each would overdose within a year. Not that it mattered now. Murphy was dead, not Peg, which meant there wouldn't be a payout.

Vader had said that after a peripheral look at the crime scene, things didn't add up. I hoped that sometime tomorrow, Zin could find out what he meant.

"Ready to head out?" Ridge asked.

"Sure," I answered, but I wasn't sure where I was going or how I'd get there. My truck was still at the main house, so that would have to be the first place I went.

"I'll stay with you tonight," Tryst said rather than asked.

"We'll be with Mom after we finish with Press and Beau," said Cru, motioning to Snapper and Kick.

Ridge gave us a lift to my mother's house, but since it was so late, we didn't go inside.

The home I lived in on the ranch now was the one my father had intended to build for my mother and him to live in. The one he'd abandoned when she told him she didn't want to move.

I didn't start building it until after he died, and it was Tryst who helped me hammer in every nail. He and I spent much of the time reminiscing about my dad, who was Tryst's older brother. He told stories about when they were kids and I wasn't around, and I told stories about my own childhood when Tryst wasn't around on a daily basis.

That was especially true when he went into the Air Force and was stationed at different bases around the world.

It was during a stint at Mexico's Military Air Base in ElCiprés that he'd traveled out of Baja California over to Sonora. There, while in search of a national park he never found, he stumbled on Alamos.

Historically, the first known records of the town dated back to 1560, when it was known as Mexico's northernmost "Silver City." Many architecturally significant buildings were constructed, along with Spanish-style mansions, from the great wealth accumulated from silver mining.

Tryst was in his early twenties when he was first enchanted by the town and purchased property there before he turned thirty.

While he hadn't spelled it out, the plan he suggested was to take Peg and Addison to his ranch in Alamos as soon as she made bail. They would be safe there in the event that either FAIM sought revenge for Murphy's death or the Killeens went after her mother or her for the money the man owed them. At the same time, it would allow us to figure out a way to either prove her innocence or that Peg shot him in self-defense.

Convincing both women to become fugitives from the law would be a challenge of epic proportions. The only way I saw them agreeing was if each believed the safety of the other necessitated it.

The next most difficult aspect was how Vader would react. He'd know where they were taken the minute he heard they were gone. Would he act on it or not? I couldn't predict one way or the other.

"You're deep in thought. Perhaps questioning what you know must be done."

"I'm in agreement, Uncle. I'm just not sure the women whose lives are at stake will also be."

"You'll present a compelling argument."

As much as I didn't want to, I had to confess what was happening. "She doesn't want to see me."

He didn't react.

"Did you already know that?"

Again, no physical reaction. "Do you know why?"

To say I did, meant suffering a level of humiliation I was unaccustomed to. "She witnessed me reacting violently to something."

"I see." Tryst's words and voice sounded just like my father's.

"I'm so ashamed."

"In her heart, Addy knows the kind of man you are. She's frightened beyond anything you or I have ever known. She'll turn to you for comfort and guidance."

"What if she doesn't?"

Trystan didn't respond even after we'd pulled up to my house and I got his bag out of the backseat of the truck's cab.

As he waited for me to unlock the north-facing front door, he ran his hand over the smooth lines of the wood. I wondered if, like me, he was thinking about the months we spent building the house my father had designed.

It was constructed in the style of homes found in Alamos: more Spanish hacienda than rural American farmhouse.

While I hadn't realized it at the time, the changes Tryst had recommended we make to my father's plans were Vastu in nature. We didn't push it as far as the houses on my uncle's ranch, but after visiting him there, I saw elements of my own home, particularly in the center room.

Rather than being a single story, like the rest of the rooms on the main level, the one I'd always considered a closed-in courtyard, was open to the second floor. A skylight in the roof bathed the space in warm light, and as per his suggestion, the room had remained empty with the exception of a single table set against the wall closest to the front door. On the opposite wall, to the north, was a five-foot square mandala wood carving, which had been a housewarming gift from Tryst.

I set my keys on the small table and took a deep breath. It had been three days since I was home for more than picking up clothes.

"I don't know about you, but I'm starving."

He nodded and raised his face to the ceiling as if there were sunlight streaming in even though it was late at night.

"Tryst?"

"Whatever you have will be fine."

I went into the kitchen and opened the refrigerator I already knew was empty. If things had gone as I'd hoped when this day began, I wouldn't have had anything to offer Addison.

Things were so much simpler just a few hours ago. While I was worried about finding Murphy, about getting the Killeens to back off on their threats, what I cared most about was spending every minute I could with Addison. Now it wasn't every moment; it was seeing her at all.

I'd never regretted my actions more than I did hitting that wall. If I could only explain my anger was at my inability to deliver on my promise to keep her safe.

I'd felt out of control, something I was never comfortable with, even as a teenager. It was the source of most disagreements between my father and me since, admittedly, we were so much alike.

I pulled a carton of eggs out of the fridge, hoping they were still fresh enough to eat, and a loaf of bread from the freezer.

"Scrambled eggs okay?" I hollered.

"Yes. Fine."

I put all twelve eggs in a bowl and whisked them, wondering if anyone had thought to ask Addison if she was hungry. The only meal either of us had eaten in the last couple of days was what my mother prepared for us earlier.

It was then that Addison had first told me to leave and take care of the things I'd neglected, but then changed her mind and said I had to eat first. Her caring about me, for me, warmed my heart. Now I wondered if she ever could again.

A minute or two after I'd dumped the eggs into a pan, my cell rang with a call from my sister.

"Is it true?" she asked before I had a chance to say hello. "Was Addy really arrested for murder?"

Either Cru, Snapper, or Kick must have told her. I wondered if my mother knew as well.

"It is true."

"Oh my God, Brix. What happened?"

I grabbed a spatula and moved the eggs around the pan. "I don't have all the details yet."

"I'm canceling the ball."

I didn't give a shit about the ball. "That's your decision."

"Maybe I'll just postpone it."

"Like I said."

"She didn't do it."

"I know, Alex."

"But Cru said she confessed."

I wished my sister had called Zin instead of me. There was no way I could reassure her when I was more worried than she was. Alex knew me well enough to call me out if she sensed I was lying. "All I can say, sis, is that the boys and I will do everything in our power to find out the truth of what happened and get Addison exonerated."

I could hear her sniffling. "I know how much you care about her, Brix."

I wondered if she truly did. Even I was stunned by the depth of what I felt for Addison.

After turning off the fire under the eggs, I told Alex I needed to go so Tryst and I could eat. She told me she'd get back to me about what she decided for the auction.

"Tell Uncle Tryst I said hello," she added before hanging up, which I passed along when he joined me in the kitchen.

"She's thinking of either postponing or canceling the Wicked Winemakers' Ball."

"You have a reprieve, then."

"How did you know I agreed to be in the bachelor auction?"

He raised a brow and took a bite of his eggs.

"Alex told you?"

Tryst nodded. "In an effort to get me to participate as well."

I had no idea how to react to that news. Was Tryst ready to start dating again? I was stunned. And if that wasn't the case, what the hell was Alex thinking?

"Does the postponement mean you have a reprieve too?"

He laughed. "I declined her invitation."

"I'm sorry, Tryst. It was thoughtless of her to ask."

"It was fine. I would just prefer not to be embarrassed when no one bids on me."

My uncle was in his late fifties and in better shape than I was. He did a workout every morning followed by yoga, then spent the rest of the day constructing new buildings or cultivating the land. I was no judge, but I would guess most women would find him very attractive.

"You'd get more bids than I would," I said before shoveling what was left of my eggs into my mouth.

"Perhaps one day we'll see."

If my mouth wasn't full, it would've dropped open. "You'd seriously do it? Be in the bachelor auction?"

He stood, took his plate to the sink, and washed the pan out. "Maybe, maybe not." After drying it, he put the pan away. "We have a very long day ahead of us tomorrow. Let's rest."

After very little sleep, but probably more than Addison got, I took a shower and put on a pair of dress pants and a collared shirt. No matter how casual the town of Cambria was, I was still entering a courtroom and would be respectful. It was another thing I'd learned from my father. While I may not always agree with "authority," those in that position deserved my respect.

When Tryst came out of the guest bedroom, I recognized the clothes he was wearing. "I hope you don't mind. I got these out of your closet while you were making dinner. I didn't bring anything appropriate to wear to court."

"It's fine," I said, smiling. "Well, almost fine. I'm annoyed that you look better in my clothes than I do."

He smirked, clearly agreeing with me. "Let's go, so we're not late."

I'd agreed to meet Zin outside of town before heading to the courthouse. When we pulled up, he was leaning against his car in the parking lot.

"Any updates?" I asked.

He shook his head. "I think it would be best if you didn't come. You either, Trystan. I can't be privy to the details of what you may or may not do once Addison is granted bail. However, if it's what I think it is, you don't want anyone to see you."

"What about the bond?"

"I'll take care of it."

Since Tryst nodded in agreement, I figured he'd already worked this out with Zin.

"What do you need from me?"

"Let someone else take charge for a change," I heard Press say from behind me.

I turned around. "Any luck with Reilly?"

"Not yet, but Snapper has a lead he's following up on. It's amazing what a cash incentive will do."

"No honor among thieves, whores, or meth heads," added Beau.

"Are we all set?" Zin asked Press.

"Do you really need to ask?" he countered, then looked over at me. "The man can't find his own arse when it's behind him, and he questions whether I am ready."

Zin flipped him off. "I was confirming, not asking."

Even I laughed at that.

"Right. Very well, then. We'll see you shortly at Seahorse," he said after Zin left for the courthouse. "The plane is fueled and ready to go."

I had to hand it to my fellow *caballeros*. They truly were prepared.

Beau Barrett used the Cessna he and Press owned jointly to travel back and forth from Napa Valley, so a plane taking off from Seahorse—with over five hundred acres and a mile of shoreline—wouldn't raise any suspicion. The aircraft had ample range to fly to Alamos and back without refueling, and with a maximum travel speed of six hundred miles per hour, we would be at the ranch in Mexico in under two.

"I should head back to Los Cab and pick up a few things." I looked at Tryst.

"My bag and yours are in the backseat of your truck."

Press raised a brow. "We should kick you out of the Caballeros for not noticing."

"Give him a pass this once," said Tryst, winking.

Less than thirty minutes later, Press joined Tryst and me as we sat on a berm, looking out at the ocean.

"It's done," he said. "Two hundred thousand."

How ironic that Addison's bail was set at the same amount Sullivan owed in gambling debts. "What happens now?"

"Zin is meeting with Peg and Addison here to talk about defense strategy."

"And what? We kidnap them?" So much for my confidence in my friends' plan.

"My plan is to lay some groundwork with Peg. It'll be up to her to convince Addy it's for their safety."

It wouldn't be an easy sell. Addison was no dummy. If she were speaking to me, I might be able to sway her, but given she'd lost all faith in me, I'd be the last person she'd listen to. To think only hours ago, I'd asked if she trusted me. Without hesitation, she'd said she did. Now, I was a person she didn't even want to see.

"Vader has requested a meeting too," said Press.

"With whom?" I asked.

"You. And by that, I mean only you."

"Where?"

"At the crime scene."

18

Brix

It was for the best that I wouldn't be at Seahorse when Addison and Peg arrived. Like before, I didn't want her to feel forced to talk to me.

I also saw Vader wanting to meet with me alone as a positive. He'd said some things didn't add up for him, and I hoped that meant he had evidence Addison didn't kill Murphy.

When I pulled up, the first thing I noticed was a familiar-looking vehicle parked across the street from Peg's house. I checked the license plate, and sure enough, it was one of our ranch trucks. What the hell was it doing here?

"Hey, Brix," Vader said, walking over to meet me. "Thanks for coming."

I'd rarely seen the man out of uniform, but today he was dressed in street clothes. Maybe because he'd been in court. I also didn't see his police cruiser. "What can I do for you, Vader, or should I say Sheriff?"

"I'm Vader this morning. Or Conrad."

I got the message. That's what Peg called him.

"Good to know."

"Let's go inside."

I stepped over the crime scene tape and waited for him to unlock the front door. "It looks pretty much like it always does," I said after surveying the living room.

"We found the body over there." He pointed in the direction of the kitchen and to a chalk outline. "And there's this." He indicated a mark on the refrigerator that looked as though it could've been left by a bullet.

"All we've recovered so far are fragments."

"Following."

He pulled a piece of paper out of his pocket and unfolded it. "You understand I am *not* showing this to you."

"Absolutely."

"This is a copy of the drawing I asked Addy to do of how it went down last night."

While the sketch was rudimentary, it was easy to see she'd entered through the back door.

"The deceased was hit twice. Both shots to the chest."

"How was the body positioned?"

"As though he'd been facing the back door."

"She didn't notice the mark on the fridge," I muttered. "There's only one other explanation, Vader. You know that."

He rested his gloved hands on the counter and hung his head. "Peg says she doesn't remember what happened. When I arrived on the scene, she was close to catatonic."

While I didn't know Addison's mother well, I had a hard time believing she'd let her only child go to prison for a crime she herself committed.

"I'm guessing the conversation you had with Peg was not in the company of an attorney."

"Why do you think you're here right now, Brix? Why I'm here? Addison couldn't have killed him if she came in through the back door."

It made sense she'd take the blame for her mother, but not that her mother would let her.

"I know what you're thinking."

"Yeah? Do you have an answer for me?"

"They both had gunshot residue on their hands. Both of their prints were on the gun. My working theory is that when Addy came in, Peg had the gun in her hand; not knowing what else to do, she grabbed the weapon and repositioned the body before we arrived."

"How long between the time you got the call until you saw her?"

"A matter of minutes."

"Wait." I picked up Addison's drawing. "If she came in through the back door, she didn't arrive here with her mother."

"Right."

I shook my head. "Vader, why the hell didn't you lead with that?"

"Because there were other things more important."

That he was right didn't lessen my frustration. What we needed to do was go back to the beginning and start over.

"So only Peg was abducted."

"Correct."

"Which means Addison somehow arrived here on her own."

I closed my eyes and nodded to myself when I realized why one of the Los Cab vehicles was out front. While it was a guess, it made sense that after seeing my display of temper, Addison took one of the ranch trucks. After all, we left the keys in them just like she did with her car. Wanting to get as far away from me as she could, she came home and stumbled on whatever was happening between her mother and stepfather.

"You said there was gunshot residue on Peg's hands?"

"Not as much as there should be."

"And Addison's?"

"Some, but less than her mother's."

As far as staging the crime scene to match the story she told, she'd failed miserably. *Thank God.*

"Addy isn't exactly a criminal mastermind," said Vader, smiling as though he'd read my thoughts. In a flash, his expression changed. "I may end up destroying my career over this, Brix, but I pray to God you already have something in mind. My gut tells me both of these women are in danger."

As an elected official, the sheriff answered to his or her constituents. If abuse of office or criminal behavior was suspected, it would be up to the state to investigate and bring charges. If we could figure out what really happened that night before Addison's next court appearance, no one would ever know she'd jumped bail. Vader would have to turn a blind eye to her and her mother's disappearance, something it sounded as though he was willing to do.

"We do have a plan," I assured him.

"Glad to hear it. If it were left to me, even with the support of the department, I'm not sure I'd be able to guarantee their safety."

"You're a good man, Conrad."

"Let's hope everyone thinks so at the end of this."

I got what he meant. I felt the same way, except I needed Addison to believe that about me *now* in order to get her to go through with what the Caballeros were planning.

"You said you fingerprinted the gun?"

Vader nodded. "Thankfully, Addy didn't have time to wipe it. We've been able to identify her prints and Peg's. It appears there's one more, but it's a partial, and we haven't had any luck getting a match on it."

"Could it be Murphy's?"

"Possibly. We should know soon."

19

Addison

"Where are we going?" my mother asked Zin when he turned in the opposite direction of her house after leaving the courthouse.

"To a friend's place for now."

I looked over the seat at her. She was rubbing her arm that still didn't have a cast on it.

"We need to get my mom back to the hospital soon."

"For?" Zin asked, looking in the rearview mirror at her.

"The doctor put her arm in a brace until the swelling went down. She's supposed to go back to have a cast put on."

His jaw visibly tightened as he digested what I'd told him. "I see."

While the judge told me the conditions of my release, everything that had happened between the time I saw

Brix punch the side of the winery building and now, was a blur.

I had no idea how long I'd be "free" and able to get my mother's life and mine in order before I was sent to prison. "I'm allowed to take her, right?"

Zin nodded, but he seemed distracted. Before I could say anything else, he drove through the gates I knew led to Seahorse Ranch.

"Why are we here?" I asked as he pulled up to a house I'd never seen before and doubted I ever would.

"We'll talk more once we're inside."

My eyes darted around the expansive drive and the parking areas near the garages. I didn't see Brix's truck or any others I'd recognize as being from Los Caballeros.

I'd made Zin give me his word that Brix wouldn't be permitted to come into the area where I'd been held at the jail. I hadn't, however, asked the attorney to assure me Brix wouldn't be waiting for me somewhere once my arraignment was over.

The idea that he wasn't there or here made my heart ache, but it didn't matter—Brix and I were finished.

Not that we'd ever really gotten started, and that was for the best.

As much as I wished things were different, they weren't, and they never could be. I *had* to stay focused on making sure everyone believed I was the one who'd killed the man I last saw in my mother's kitchen. As long as I could do that, everything would be fine.

20
Brix

We've arrived at Seahorse, said the text I received from Zin.

On my way, I responded.

"Everything okay?" Vader asked.

"If there isn't anything else, I need to get going."

"Nothing I can think of right now."

"Use Timebomb if you need to reach me." The app automatically deleted messages within a few seconds of them being read, and they didn't show up in the first place without the receiver entering a secret code to view them.

"Roger that."

I pulled up and parked my truck next to Zin's vehicle. Sometime later today, Snapper and Kick would pick it up and take it back to Los Cab.

I couldn't remember a time in my life when I felt more anxious than I did right now. Rather than getting out right away, I stayed in the driver's seat of the cab and took several deep breaths. I wanted Addison to be in my life, no matter what our relationship turned out to be. If all she wanted was my friendship, I'd respect her decision regardless of how difficult it would be for me. The only thing I couldn't accept was her shutting me out. I'd beg her to let me explain what she'd seen, if it came to that. I'd get down on my knees and plead if necessary.

I knew her heart. I'd known it since shortly after I met her. Addison was incapable of cruelty; she didn't have a mean bone in her body. If I begged, she'd relent.

She also wasn't capable of murder.

I slowly opened the truck door and climbed out. My feet grew heavier with every step I took toward the main entrance to the house.

When I saw the light near the top right of the door change from red to green, I grabbed the handle and walked over the threshold. Zin, Peg, and Addison were sitting in the living room, and all three raised their heads. My eyes met those of the woman who held my heart, and I watched as hers filled with tears.

I longed to rush over, pull her into my arms, and soothe her pain, her confusion, her fear, but would she let me? I took measured steps, closing the distance between us.

As I drew nearer, her eyes widened.

"Addison," I whispered. It became a plea when I held my hand out to her. I didn't move close enough that she could take it until I saw her arm raise. With one more step, I grasped her hand in mine, pulled her from the sofa where she sat, and held her in my arms. "I've missed you so much," I said, resting my cheek against her hair. I felt her breath hitch and placed my hand on the back of her head.

"Will you excuse us?" I said to Zin and Peg. When the two stood and left the room, I sat on the sofa and pulled Addison onto my lap.

"I'm too heavy," she mumbled, trying to scoot away, but I wouldn't let her.

"Let me hold you, baby." Her tension eased, and her body settled into mine. God, I loved the feel of her in my arms.

I put my fingers on her chin to turn her head to kiss her and felt her tension return. She wriggled from my grasp, and this time, I let her go.

"I can't do this." Her eyes darted around the room as though she was looking for a way to escape.

"Addison, please look at me."

She folded her arms and looked out at the ocean instead.

"Before I came inside, I vowed that, if necessary, I'd beg you to give me the opportunity to explain what you saw."

"It doesn't matter."

"It matters to me. Everything about you matters."

She shook her head as tears ran down her face. "You need to let go, Brix."

"Of you? Never." It wasn't a matter of choice. I could no more walk away from Addison Reagan than I could rip my own heart from my chest.

"I'm going to prison."

"What for, Addison?"

When she shook her head, I knew Zin was right when he said he believed her request not to see me was more about her inability to lie to me about killing Murphy. I stepped right in front of her, put my hands on her shoulders, and stared into her eyes.

"What for, Addison?"

"Murphy is dead."

"That isn't what I asked. Why are you going to prison?"

"That is why." When she tried to look away, I put my hands on either side of her face.

"Tell me the truth."

"Leave me alone, Brix. I'm begging you."

"Don't you think I already know the truth?"

"Don't do this!" she shouted.

Her stubbornness was baffling, which meant I didn't understand what was motivating her. "Tell me why not."

"Because nothing will change the fact that he's dead, and I'm going to prison for killing him."

I lowered my voice when she raised hers more. "We both know you didn't do it."

"I'm sorry to interrupt, but it's time," I heard my uncle say.

"Not yet."

"No, Brix. We must leave now," Tryst insisted.

"You're leaving?"

"*We're* leaving." I removed my hands from her face and put my arm around her shoulders. "Let's go."

Addison stopped walking and folded her arms. "Where are you taking me?"

"Somewhere you'll be safe."

Her eyes opened wide. "What about my mother?"

"She's going too."

"Gabriel, we must leave *now*," Tryst pressed for the second time.

I cupped Addison's face. "You said once that you trusted me. I need you to do that now, baby. If you will, I promise I won't ask any more questions."

"But—"

I felt my own eyes filling with tears of frustration. I couldn't force her onto the plane that would deliver her and her mother to a place where they could be kept safe until we figured out who'd actually killed Murphy. I knew Addison hadn't, and something in my gut told me Peg hadn't either.

"What if I don't go with you? Will you go with Trystan?"

Her eyes bored into mine, and she slowly shook her head.

"Addy?" I heard Peg say from beside me. "Please, sweetheart."

She looked between her mother and me, then nodded as slowly as she'd just shook her head.

I didn't hesitate. I took her hand and led her outside, where Beau and Press were waiting in the cockpit of the private plane. Once they delivered us to Alamos, they would return to Cambria and resume their search, along with Snapper and Kick, for Reilly, who we all believed held the answers we sought. At least some of them.

"Mama?" I said, stunned to see her already seated on the plane when we entered the cabin.

"Hello, *mijo*." She smiled and hugged her purse closer to her belly. My mother wasn't a fan of flying, particularly in a plane this small.

"I thought it best we ask Lucia to join us," said Trystan, more to Peg than to me.

"Thank you," I heard her murmur before she took the seat next to my mom.

"How's this?" I said to Addison, pointing to two seats a couple of rows farther back.

"It's fine."

I wove my fingers with hers as she silently sat beside me. I told her that if she would trust me, I wouldn't ask any more questions. It was a promise I had no idea how I'd keep.

21

Brix

Given I knew with everything in me that Addison hadn't killed Murphy, her responses, reactions, even her demeanor before my uncle insisted we leave, made no sense to me.

When I looked over at her, she squeezed my hand, but a split second later, the tension flowing from her body into mine was strong enough that I felt my breath catch.

When my innate response bordered on demanding she tell me the truth—even though I'd just told her I wouldn't—I did the only other thing I knew could harness my reaction. I wove the fingers of one hand into her hair, held tight, and ground my lips to hers.

The kiss was everything but gentle. I pushed my tongue into her mouth and pressed hard enough that her head was forced up against the back of her seat.

Her whimper made me want to possess her more. Only when I felt her succumb, kiss me back, did I ease off and make love to her mouth instead. I nibbled her lower lip, soothed the sting with my own, and wound her tongue with mine. I dropped my hand and rested it against her heart. I could feel her pebbled nipple beneath my palm, but that wasn't what I craved. I wanted to feel her heart beating, know that my mouth on hers was affecting her as powerfully as it was me.

When the plane's wheels hit the ranch's airstrip, I rested my forehead against hers.

"I wish—"

Addison silenced me with her fingertips on the lips that had just ravished hers. I was about to speak again, but when she turned her head away, I remained silent.

"Where are we?" Peg asked when the plane came to a stop.

"Welcome to my ranch, *El Lugar de Curación*, or in English, the Healing Place," he answered.

I prayed that whatever had traumatized Addison would heal while we were here. It wasn't that she'd killed Murphy because I *knew* she hadn't. Something told me her mother hadn't either. Which could only mean that whoever had, was responsible not just for her behavior, but her confession too. It was the only explanation that made sense.

When we exited the plane, we were greeted by a man I didn't recognize, who pulled up in a golf cart.

"This is David," Tryst said before introducing each of us to the man, who nodded but didn't speak. "He'll take you to your *casitas*."

When the golf cart driver pulled up to the first *casita*, I got out to unload the bags. He took Peg's and my mom's, but when I grabbed Addison's, he shook his head.

I sent Tryst a text. *Is the driver mistaken? Isn't Addison supposed to stay with Peg and my mom?*

His response was simple. *He is not mistaken.*

"What's going on?" Addison asked when I scrubbed my face with my hand. "Am I staying with you?"

"I'm sorry about this. I don't know what my uncle's thinking."

"If you don't want me—"

"Stop right there. I want more than anything for us to have time alone together. I just don't want you to feel uncomfortable."

"I won't."

"If you're sure."

"Brix—"

I shook my head and put my fingertips on her lips. *"Llévanos al templo, por favor."*

David nodded and turned the cart in the opposite direction.

"Why are we going to a temple?" Addison asked, making me smile. So much for trying to surprise her.

"It's the most beautiful place on the whole ranch and the first building I want you to set foot in."

"Why?"

"You'll see."

"I'll take your bags to the sunrise *casita*," said the driver when he pulled up to the sacred structure.

"I didn't think you spoke English. Actually, I wondered if you spoke at all."

"I don't like talking." He shrugged and drove away.

"Strange man," murmured Addison, smiling for the first time since I arrived at Seahorse this morning.

I caressed her face. "I love seeing your smile. I've missed it."

Surprising me, she leaned into my hand and closed her eyes.

"I wish I knew what you were thinking," I whispered.

"Can we go inside?"

We walked up the steps made of large stones set in concrete that matched the temple's foundation. I pulled open the wooden door set into the brick that formed the building's walls and lined the inside of the conical-shaped ceiling—the outside of which was covered in cement that looked almost like marble.

"Wait," she said, standing in the doorway. She closed her eyes, took three deep breaths, and let them out slowly. "Okay. I'm ready."

Like the ceiling, the altar—also called a mandir—was conical-shaped and was constructed of sandalwood. On it sat several murtis, or statues of gods, illuminated by subdued lamps made to look like candlelight.

When Addison stepped into the center of the temple, under the small skylights built into the steeple, it was as though the sun broke out of the clouds just to shine on her. When she raised her face, the rays bathed her in a light like none I'd ever seen. It was as though the central energy field my uncle so often spoke of—Brahma, the Creator—swirled around her. Tears streamed down her face, but she was smiling. She slowly spun in a circle as though she was allowing the light to rinse away all her pain, all her sadness, all her fear, like water from a shower.

I watched her for several minutes, mesmerized, until the sun went behind a cloud and the magic ended.

Addison's eyes opened, and her gaze met mine. "What just happened?"

"If my uncle were here, my guess is he'd say you experienced enlightenment."

"It was so warm. I hadn't even realized I was cold."

She looked around her as though she was seeing the rest of the space for the first time. "What do all these mean?" she asked, motioning to the various statues that sat on shelves around the room in addition to on the altar.

"Tryst would be a better person to ask. I only remember one." I pointed to the figure with four heads and four sets of hands. "That's Brahma, aka the creator." The same god I thought of when Addison was bathed in sunlight.

I watched as she walked around the space, studying each of the deities. The tension that had been so evident earlier seemed to have melted away and left serenity in its place.

"Brix?" She stepped closer and held both of my hands in hers.

"Yeah, baby?"

"No matter what happens, I want you to know that bringing me here was the greatest gift you could have given me."

I hated that she sounded resigned after what I'd hoped was an awakening that would lead to her telling me the truth about how Murphy died. Instead, I felt defeated. Addison's ruse remained firmly in place, which meant the Caballeros and I would be forced to find out what happened on our own.

"Would you prefer I switched *casitas* with your mom?" I asked as we walked out of the temple.

She folded her arms and stared at me. "I wouldn't."

I held up both my hands. "Believe me, it isn't what I want either. I was just trying to be a gentleman."

"Stop that."

"Stop what?"

"Trying. Just be who you are."

Her words frustrated me. "Is that what you're doing? Being who you are?"

"What do you mean?"

"The Addison I know isn't capable of lying."

"Maybe you don't know me as well as you think."

I softened my tone. "But I do, baby. I know you better than anyone."

Her eyes filled with tears like they had so many times since this morning, and she shook her head.

"I do and you know it. There isn't another living soul who has spent years paying attention to you in the way I have. You wanna know how I know?" I didn't wait for an answer. "Because I would've noticed that too." I put my arms around her and looked up at the sky. "I'm going to tell you something else I'm not proud of, but I also eavesdropped on your conversations sometimes when you didn't know I was there."

"You did?"

"Yes. And what I learned was the person you are when no one's looking is the same person you are when everyone is. I *know* you didn't kill Murphy, Addison. What I don't know is why you confessed to a crime you didn't commit."

Her inability to lie was written all over her face. She bit her bottom lip and averted her eyes.

"Is it because you think your mother killed him?"

When she looked as though she was about to flee, I put my arm around her waist and pulled her close to me.

"Don't you know by now I would do anything for you, Addison? *Anything*."

"Don't do this, Brix," she cried.

"Do what? Beg you to tell me the truth so I can help you?"

Rather than waiting for her to answer, I scooped her into my arms and carried her to the *casita* that was only a few yards away. With every step I took, she cried harder. I wanted her to talk to me, to tell me the truth, but not until she released all the emotion that was breaking her apart, turning her into someone she wasn't.

Like when the sun's light had washed over her in the temple, I believed her tears would cleanse her too. I didn't try to comfort or soothe her beyond holding her body close to mine. I wanted her to get it out, not keep anything inside.

With one hand, I opened the door to the small house, then carried her through the main room to the back, where the larger of the two bedrooms was. Without releasing her from my arms, I lay on the bed.

When her tears subsided, I stroked her hair but didn't speak. I wanted her to tell me what happened without my questioning her. There was no hurry. With nowhere to go and nothing we had to do, I could wait all night. Longer, if necessary.

"I'm scared," she whispered.

I was about to say I was too, when I realized it might be me causing her fear. We still hadn't talked about what she saw at the winery. I took a deep breath and let it out slowly. "I promised you I'd keep you safe, and you said you trusted me. Then I destroyed it. What you saw…"

"You don't need to explain," she whispered.

"But I do. I'm sure this will come as a surprise to you, but I'm a bit of a control freak." I winked and saw a slight smile. "I was attempting to make a deal with the people Murphy owed money to. They weren't interested, and I didn't understand why not. It was my frustration over my inability to keep my promise that made me react in a way that is out of character for me."

Her eyes studied mine. "Brix…"

"I'm sorry, Addison, and I hope you'll forgive me. I know it's too much to expect you to trust me after what you witnessed."

"I do trust you."

"Just not enough to tell me the truth."

"It doesn't matter."

"Of course it does."

She shook her head. "I confessed."

"There's still an investigation into the crime, even when someone confesses. There may not be sufficient evidence to support the confession, or there may be evidence that someone else committed the crime."

Addison turned pale.

"One way or another, I'm going to help you, protect you, baby. It would be so much easier if you'd just tell me what really happened."

"What if I don't know?"

I forced myself to hold in the sigh of relief that she was finally talking to me. "Tell me everything you do know."

22

Addison

Brix wanted me to relive the worst night of my life. Not only that, in order to tell him what he wanted to know, I'd have to betray my mother.

But how could I tell him what happened when I didn't understand it myself?

I'd just said I trusted him, but did I really? With my own life, yes. With my mother's? That, I wasn't certain of.

Brix stroked my cheek with his finger. "Addison?"

He was so close. Too close, but at the same time, I felt such a sense of relief being in his arms.

"I don't know where to start."

"How about what you did after you saw me punch a brick wall with my bare hand?"

I smiled because he was, but what I would give to rewind the clock to that day, and instead of running away, go to him and ask what was wrong. But would I really have? First, I doubted I'd be brave enough.

Second, if I was granted that wish, there was a good chance my mother would be dead.

"I won't lie; I was upset. What I saw was so out of character for you."

His eyes lowered. "I wish I could take it back," he whispered.

I ran my finger down his cheek like he'd just done to me. "You said you hoped I'd forgive you, but, Brix, you need to forgive yourself."

He shook his head. "The chain of events that was set in motion…"

"I thought about that too. What if I could go back and do it differently, and you know what? If I could, my mother and I might be dead."

He shuddered and tightened his hold on me. "Addison, please tell me what happened when you got to your mother's house."

I nodded and rolled my shoulders. "I jumped in one of the Los Cab trucks. At that point, I wasn't even thinking. I was on autopilot. I drove home out of instinct, I guess, and when I arrived, lights were on. As I got closer to the back door, I could hear my mother's voice from inside." I closed my eyes when I felt a wave of nausea. "Then I heard gunshots. Two of them."

Brix nodded.

"Looking back on it, I was an idiot for going in, but like I said, I wasn't thinking. I raced in the back door and saw Dennis' body on the floor. My mother was standing over him, staring at the gun in her hand and sobbing."

"Which hand?"

I had to think about it for a minute. "Her right."

"Did it seem like she was in any physical pain?"

"What do you mean?"

"Rubbing her arm, cradling it, anything like that?"

"She was crying, more like keening, but I don't remember her doing that."

"What happened next?"

"I didn't know what to do. I ran over and took the gun from her. By then she was sobbing incoherently, so I got her over to the chair. She was rocking back and forth, and I felt like she was trying to tell me something. That's when I heard the sirens and set the gun on the counter."

"Where was Dennis' body?"

"On the kitchen floor."

"You moved him."

"Yes. I pulled his feet and turned his body so it looked like he'd been facing the back door."

"Is that when Vader arrived?"

"It is, along with two deputies."

"And you told him you'd killed Dennis."

"You didn't see her, Brix. I didn't know what else to do. At first she was crying so hard, then all of a sudden, she stopped. She went so still, so pale. For a second, I thought she'd died too."

"Catatonic," he said quietly.

"Right. That's how she seemed."

"You said you thought she was trying to tell you something. When I got to the police station, I saw you. Her and you. Your mom looked distraught, but certainly not catatonic."

"It was Vader's presence that made her come out of it. The first thing he did was tell me not to say another word. Then he walked over and knelt in front of her. She didn't look at him at first, but when he put his hand on her arm, she started to cry again."

"Did she say anything?"

"I think she may have wanted to, but he told her not to try to speak."

"What happened next?"

"After talking to the deputies for a few minutes, Vader took her and me to the police station. It wasn't long before Zin arrived and Mom and I were separated. I was so worried about her."

"Is that when Vader interviewed you?"

"He asked a few questions, told me to draw what happened. Zin protested at first, but I had already confessed."

"Did you see or hear anything—*anyone*—else? Besides Vader and the deputies?"

I shook my head. "Not that I remember. It all happened so fast. I guess I just reacted out of instinct."

"During the interview, did you tell Vader you shot Dennis?"

Tears streamed down my face. "If you'd seen her," I repeated. "I had to. After all she went through, and I didn't—" I was crying too hard to say anything more.

Brix stroked my hair and told me to let it out.

"You said that even though I confessed, there would still be an investigation. I can't let her go to prison. She's already endured so much."

"She won't, baby."

"How do you know?"

"Because your mother didn't kill Murphy. She couldn't have."

"How can you be sure?"

"She couldn't have fired a gun of that caliber, especially twice. Once, maybe."

"Even if she feared for her life?"

"While it doesn't mean he wasn't threatening her, Vader said Murphy was unarmed."

Just saying that she couldn't fire the gun, didn't seem like enough to me. "When in fear, especially for their lives, don't people get surges of adrenaline that result in them doing things that might seem impossible?"

"Yes, that's possible, but there's more."

"What?"

"There were traces of gunshot residue on your mother's hand, but not the amount that should've been if she'd pulled the trigger. It was the same with yours."

"I don't remember them checking."

"Were you fingerprinted?"

"Yes, but it's a blur."

"Vader said there was a third print on the gun. It was partial, but he's hoping it's enough to get a match."

"I didn't even know my mother had a gun."

"I'm sure the sheriff is checking into that too."

I took a deep breath as the ramifications of my confession, along with Brix saying my mother couldn't have killed Dennis, sank in. If neither of us killed him, who did?

23

Brix

I didn't want to let Addison go or get up from the bed we were lying on, but I needed to pass everything I'd just learned on to someone. Ridge, at least. He could inform Vader and the other *caballeros*.

While it wasn't much more than we'd already surmised, having her accounting might give us more clues.

Addison shivered, and I rubbed my hand down her arm. "What was that?"

"Do you think whoever killed Dennis was in the house the whole time?"

"Not likely. I'm sure that after Vader took you to the station, the deputies checked out the rest of the house."

I was just about to tell her I needed to make a phone call when Addison shocked all thoughts straight out of my head. At least the one sitting on my shoulders. She moved her hand down my body and cupped my crotch.

"Addison?"

"There's something else I need to talk to you about."

"Um, okay."

She rolled her eyes, something I was happy to see rather than the sadness that had been ever present. I studied her, and she bit her lip.

"Brix. I want to sleep with you."

Admittedly, I was stunned by her candor. I shouldn't have been, given her palm was massaging my quickly growing erection.

Addison flushed. "What I should've said was that I want to have sex."

"Um, okay," I repeated.

"I can't believe I actually told you that," she muttered.

While every part of my body other than my brain was on board, like before, I wasn't ready to let go of the fantasy of the first time we made love being in a tree house overlooking the ocean.

She rolled so her back was to me. "Look, under other circumstances, I would be mortified by your lack of enthusiasm and tell you to forget I said anything. But I can't do that. I know you said there would be an investigation, but I confessed, which means there's a chance I'll still go to prison. Before that happens, I want to have sex. With you."

"Thanks for adding that last bit," I mumbled.

"You knew that's what I meant."

She peered over her shoulder when I sighed and scrubbed my face with my hand. "Are you mad at me?"

"I have a lot of feelings for you swirling around inside of me, Addison. Anger isn't one of them."

"But—"

"Look at me." She rolled so she was on her back. I lifted my body, urged her legs open with my knee, put my hands on either side of her, leaned down, and kissed her. I stroked her hair with one hand, took a short break from her mouth, and moved my lips to her forehead, her eyelids, and down to the place right beneath her ear.

She shuddered when I kept going, unfastening the buttons on her blouse as I moved down the body I'd longed to possess for longer than I even remembered.

Addison Reagan had crawled right under my skin the very first time I saw her smile.

"Sit up for me." I helped remove her top, tossed it to the floor, then reached behind and unclasped her bra. The cups fell forward, and it ended up on the floor too.

Without hesitation, I sucked one nipple until she cried out for more, and I switched sides.

"I want these off," I told her when I released the button on her jeans, not that I intended to wait for her to remove them. I unfastened the zipper and reached inside, sliding my hand under her panties and cupping her ass. While we wouldn't be fulfilling her fantasy today, we sure as hell would be some of mine.

I had longed to get my hands on her ass, her tits, her pussy, every part of her to the point where the idea of having sex with anyone else disgusted me. I wanted Addison. No one but her.

I slid my hand out, shifted off the bed so I was standing, and pulled her to the end so her legs dangled and her feet could touch the floor. Only then did I pull down her pants and throw them, along with her panties, on the floor with the rest of her clothes.

"God, you're beautiful." I looked up and down her body, and when she tried to cover herself, I grabbed both of her wrists. "Don't. I want to look at you. Let me see more." I spread her legs wider. "I need a taste."

I sank to my knees and licked through her folds, exploring her pussy with my tongue and paying careful attention to her clit.

Addison wove her fingers in my hair as I continued licking, sucking, swirling her hardened nub with the tip of my tongue. When I felt her body tense, I thrust two fingers deep inside her.

"Brix—" She arched her back, closed her eyes tight, and let out the sexiest sound I'd ever heard.

I felt her clench. "Let go, baby."

My name on her lips as she writhed in pleasure, nearly unhinged me. I moved my clothed body up her naked one and pulled her into my arms. I grabbed her hand when I felt her fingers back on the waistband of my jeans.

"I want to look at you too," she whined.

"I need to ask you something first."

She pulled away, and I let her. "I know what you're going to say."

I raised a brow. "Can I say it anyway?"

"I can't stop you."

"If you didn't believe you were going to prison, would you still want this to happen between us now? Keyword being *now*."

"I can't tell you how I'd feel. I know I want to have sex with you." She rested her head back on my chest. "If you don't…want to go any further, I understand."

I moved her hand that rested on my waistband and put it on my erection. "Evidence of how much I want to." I put her hand back on my chest. "What I'm saying is, this—you—mean something to me, Addison. While the words you used were 'have sex,' the words I'd use are different."

Before I could say anything else, my cell rang with a tone I recognized. "I'm sorry. The timing couldn't be worse, but I have to take this, Addison."

I nearly cursed my best friend when she nodded and got up as I reached for my phone.

"Hey, Ridge. Do you have any news for me?" I asked when I picked up the call.

"I do, and I'm afraid it isn't the good kind, Brix."

"What?"

"I've already been in touch with Tryst, but there's a new female prosecutor sniffing around. She's been asking about a deposition." Shit, that meant Vader wasn't able to keep Addison off the court's radar in the way we'd hoped he'd be able to.

"Is Zin handling it?"

"As best as he can."

"You said she's new."

"Yep. Seraphina Reeve, and whatever you do, don't call her Sara."

"I take it you've spoken with her?"

"Only briefly."

"Is there any progress on finding Reilly?"

"Nada."

"Up your efforts."

"We're throwing everything at this, Brix."

"Not enough if you haven't found him yet."

"I'll let the guys know."

"If there's nothing else, I was going to call you in a little while with news of my own."

"Yeah?"

My eyes met Addison's when she came back into the room. "Neither Addison nor her mother killed Murphy."

"That isn't exactly news, Brix, but since you're reporting it that way, does that mean Addy recanted?"

I held my hand out to her and pulled her back down on the bed. "She told me what happened that night, so, yes."

"Does she know who did kill him?"

Her eyes bored into mine. "Negative."

"And she didn't see or hear anything that might give us a clue?"

She shook her head.

"Negative on that too."

"What do you want me to do with this information?"

"Share it with Vader, then fucking find Reilly."

"We're on it, Brix. Full throttle."

"Also, up security at Los Cab. Whoever the real killer is doesn't know for certain whether Addison saw anything."

"What about her mother?"

"I haven't had a chance to talk to her yet, but I will soon."

"Copy that, and as far as security goes at Los Cab, it's about as tight as we can get it, especially at this time of year, but I'll talk to Trevino about the potential of a higher-level threat."

"Bring Burns in on it too."

Ridge laughed. "Sorcha may send out a search party soon; that's how much time he's been spending here."

"Glad to hear it."

"Anything else?" he asked.

"Not for now. Just *find* Reilly."

I ended the call and looked into Addison's wide eyes. Her face was ghostly pale again.

"Talk to me."

She put her hand on her stomach almost as if she was about to be sick. "You just told Ridge I wasn't the killer."

"First of all, everyone who knows you never believed you were. Second, I trust Ridge with my life, and you should too."

"I hope you're right," she mumbled.

"I am, Addison. I also predict that once the Caballeros find Reilly, it won't be long before we catch the real killer."

"Who is Reilly?"

"He worked at Los Cab for a while. We believe he had something to do with your mother's abduction."

"I always wondered if they were real."

"If you mean Los Caballeros, it is." I'd spent so much of my life knowing I could never divulge the secret society to anyone. I was surprised how easy it was to admit it to Addison. "I wasn't supposed to tell you that."

"No? I told you something I probably never should have, either."

I'd say we were even, but there was nothing to tease about what she shared with me. I would let Tryst know that I'd told her, however, and probably Ridge too.

"Brix?"

"Yeah, baby?"

"We never finished our conversation from earlier. You know, about sex."

"Making love."

"I never knew you were such a romantic."

"I'm not sure I was. Or that I am." I cupped her face and stared into her eyes. "I told you how important you are to me, Addison. I meant that. I won't lie and tell you I haven't had sex before, but I will tell you there hasn't been a single person I've made love to."

"Brix...I..."

"If it isn't as important to you as it is to me, I'll understand." I was about to say that if it wasn't, nothing more would be happening between us, but could I stop myself from touching her if we spent every night in bed together? Even if I lied to myself and said I could, I doubted I could keep myself from giving in to the sweet temptation I craved.

The one thing I could say for certain was there was a line I couldn't cross with her. Until I knew Addison felt as strongly about me as I did her, we could touch, kiss, pleasure each other with our hands and mouths, but that would be all.

Maybe I was more of a romantic than I'd ever admitted to myself because I couldn't get the idea that our first time was in her fantasy tree house out of my head.

Before I could say any of that, my cell rang, this time with a call from Kick. "I'm sorry, this one is important too."

Addison motioned with her hand for me to answer.

"Any luck?" I asked rather than saying hello.

"We found Reilly."

I let out a sigh of relief. I was convinced he was the key to finding the real killer.

24

Addison

I was standing close enough to Brix to hear his conversation clearly.

"Kick, listen to me. There is a lot of information we want him to give up, and that means keeping him alive," he said.

"Can I kill him once he's told us everything he knows?" I really didn't need to hear *that*. Was Brix's brother serious?

"Not funny, Kick."

"Spoilsport. There's a glitch, though."

Brix sighed.

"He's saying he'll only talk to you."

"No way. He's not in a position to make demands. Go ahead and tell him I said you could kill him if he doesn't talk. Better yet, tell him I said Cru could do it."

"Roger that."

Rather than listen any more, I left the room. I was headed to the kitchen when the light streaming in through the skylights in what Brix had called the main room beckoned me.

I'd never felt anything as powerful as when I stood in the temple and light coming in through the skylights warmed me. I truly did feel like I experienced enlightenment, like Brix had suggested Tryst would say. It was as if I had perfect clarity in every aspect of my life. I *knew* I had to tell Brix the truth about what had happened the night of Dennis' death. The only problem was, once the light went behind a cloud, my bravery went with it.

Now, though, I felt such a sense of relief. Brix knew what had happened, and he'd help me, just like he'd promised.

Desperately wanting to experience that feeling again, I stood under the light with my palms open.

After several seconds, I realized what I felt now was peace more than clarity. Rather than knowing what I needed to do, I felt as if the light was wrapping me in a loving hug. I sighed in happiness.

When I turned and opened my eyes, Brix was crouched near the doorway.

"Hi."

He stood, closed the distance between us, and pulled me close. "Hi, baby."

I leaned into him like a cat. "What happens now?"

"How about we go for a walk?"

"I'd like that." I looked down at my bare feet. "Better get shoes."

He smiled. "While you do, I'm going to send Tryst a text. I need to get him caught up."

I bit my lower lip. "Are you sure my mom couldn't have killed Dennis?"

"Positive. However, it's imperative we get her to tell us what happened prior to him being shot and you arriving."

"She hasn't wanted to talk about it." Something occurred to me. "We should take her to the temple."

"Yeah?"

"Being there helped me realize I had to tell you the truth. Maybe it'll inspire her to do the same. Unless your mother has already convinced her." Even to myself, I sounded *Pollyanna-ish*, but I truly believed what I'd experienced was that powerful.

"My uncle is on his way," Brix said when I met him outside the front door. "In fact, there he is now." He pointed to Tryst, who was riding toward us on a horse. "Do you ride?"

Ride? Seriously? I didn't have time to go for a walk most days; how was I supposed to fit in horseback riding? And even if I had time, I certainly couldn't afford to do it. I wondered if Brix realized the full extent of what we didn't have in common. Once he got a bigger taste of how far on the other side of the tracks I came from, maybe I wouldn't mean quite as much to him as he thought.

"Addison?"

I shook my head. "No, I've never ridden a horse."

His smile disarmed me. "Would you like to?"

What the hell? We were on a ranch, right? I could at least try it. "I would."

His smile grew wider. "I'm so glad."

"I'm happy to see you're both having a nice afternoon," Tryst said, getting off his horse.

"Addison and I would like to go for a ride when it's convenient."

"That can certainly be arranged. I have several horses in my stable that would suit you both quite well."

Brix took the reins from him and tied the animal off on the railing of the porch.

"You said we needed to talk." Tryst motioned to the front door. "Shall we go inside?"

I walked in first when Brix held the door open for me, and went to sit in the living room, only realizing after I'd taken a seat that maybe the two men wanted to talk privately. "Should I excuse myself?" I asked.

Brix shook his head, sat beside me, and covered my hand with his.

"First, I need you to know I confirmed Addison's question this morning when she asked if Los Caballeros is real."

Tryst slowly nodded. "It was to be expected."

Brix's eyes opened wide. "What do you mean?"

"Every *caballero* eventually confides in the one person they're unable to keep secrets from. That yours would be Addy will come as a surprise to no one." Tryst leaned forward. "I sense there is something more important you would like me to know."

Brix turned to me. "Would you prefer to tell him or…"

"I will." I took a deep breath. "While I confessed, you should know I didn't kill my stepfather."

Tryst nodded in the same way he had when Brix'd told him I knew about Los Caballeros—as if what I'd told him wasn't news.

"I don't think my mother did, either."

"Nor do I."

"But I don't know who did."

He looked between Brix and me. "I believe that is something the *caballeros* are trying to determine as we speak."

"Addison, would you mind repeating what you told me about the chain of events the night Dennis was shot?"

I'd said it all out loud once, so I could again. Something told me it wouldn't be the last time I did.

Tryst sat back in his chair and steepled his fingers in front of his mouth. "The question now is who would want Murphy dead?"

"I'm hoping Reilly can give us some insight that will lead to the answer to that question," said Brix. "Addison suggested we invite her mother to join us at the temple."

Tryst turned his head so his eyes met mine. "I concur."

25
Brix

While Tryst and Addison continued their conversation, I focused on who may have wanted Murphy dead. Logically, it was neither the Killeens nor FAIM.

The Killeens wanted their money, which they'd never get if he was dead. If our theories were correct, FAIM wanted their money too, at least those he'd coerced into helping him. If anything, they would've killed Peg, not her husband.

Unless—I tapped my cheek with my index finger—whoever was at Peg's house at the time of the murder wanted Dennis dead more than they wanted a piece of the life insurance payout.

I didn't know exactly who was questioning Reilly, and it would be prudent to wait to call Ridge until after we'd talked to Peg. Instead, I sent him a message via Timebomb.

See if Reilly knows of anyone in or out of FAIM who wanted Murphy dead.

I waited until I saw the message had been delivered before tucking my phone in my back pocket.

"Ready?" Tryst asked.

When I nodded and followed him and Addison outside, I saw David was back with the golf cart. I overheard my uncle ask him to return his horse to the stables and tell him we would be using the cart.

David nodded but, like before, didn't speak.

"He's an odd one," I mumbled, sitting in the second-row seat. Rather than sit next to Tryst up front, Addison climbed in beside me. I took her hand in mine when I saw it was shaking. "I know this is difficult."

She looked out at the horizon. "I'm scared, Brix, and I'm sure my mom is too. I just don't see a way out of spending my life in prison other than finding the real killer."

"Innocent until proven guilty, baby, and you won't be. There is no evidence to support your confession."

She nodded. "I know that's what you said, but even if that's true, I would still worry about the person who shot Dennis coming after my mom or me."

It was a valid fear, and one I shared. I doubted many people in the world cared whether Murphy was dead or alive. There were, however, people who would want to stop Addison or her mom from talking if they had, in fact, seen something.

Tryst drove to the *casita* where Peg and my mother were staying, walked to the door, and knocked. When my mom answered, I heard him tell her we were going to the temple and hoped they would join us.

A few seconds later, both women followed him over to the three-row cart.

"No, *mijo*, stay put," my mother said when I got up to move to the row of seats farthest back. "It's a short drive."

The whole way, she chattered about the ranch and how much she missed spending time here. Given her general fear of flying, I wondered whether she would if she had the opportunity to visit more often.

"There it is," she exclaimed when we drove up. "It's even more beautiful than I remembered."

I held back when I saw Addison put her arm through her mother's left one as they both got out of the cart. "Wait until you see inside," I heard her say.

"Mama," I said when she went to follow them. "Let's give them some time on their own."

She looked at Tryst, who nodded and motioned her farther away from the building. I joined them.

"We believe there was someone else at Peg's house the night Murphy was murdered, and whoever that person is, is the real killer."

My mother's eyes hooded, but she nodded.

"Has Peg said anything at all about what happened that night?"

"Nothing, but I sense there is much fermenting beneath the surface."

"Mama," I scolded.

"So what if I use a winemaking phrase? It is still the truth."

"Not the point, and you know it." I sat down on the backseat of the cart and looked over at the temple. "Addison had a moment when we were here."

"A moment?" asked my mother.

I looked over at Tryst. "It was a beautiful thing to see."

He smiled, and I could swear he blinked away tears.

"She's hoping the same happens with her mom."

"I pray she's right," he said, raising his face to the sun.

When we saw the doors open a few minutes later, all three of us walked over to join them. I was within a foot of her when my cell rang with a call I knew was from Ridge.

I held up my index finger, and Addison nodded.

"Hey, have you managed to get anything out of Reilly?"

"Negative. He's still pretty amped-up on meth. However, Press received news about Murphy's identity."

I closed my eyes and listened as what Ridge told me made the pit in my stomach grow into a boulder.

"Is there anything else?" I asked when he finished telling me things I wished he hadn't.

"Not yet. I'll let you know as soon as Reilly is coherent. Do you want me to brief Tryst, or will you?"

"You do it."

I ended the call and put my cell in my back pocket. Addison walked in my direction at the same time Tryst walked farther away and answered his own phone.

"What's happened?" she asked.

"There's no easy answer to that question. I can tell you this much. We believe we have a lead on Murphy's killer." I reached out and caught her when she turned pale and looked like she was about to pass out. I helped her over to the golf cart.

"Who is it?"

I put my hands on her shoulders and looked into her eyes. "Trust me when I say this is a conversation I need to have with your mother first."

She gasped. "Oh my God! I thought you said you were sure she didn't kill him."

"No, no. Shit. I'm sorry. That came out wrong." I sat beside her. "We need to know what your mom saw that night. You said you heard her talking to someone, right?"

"Her voice, yes."

"I have to find out who that was."

"I assumed it was Dennis."

I didn't want to think about the ramifications for Peg if it wasn't.

26
Addison

"Don't."

"I'm sorry?"

I put my hand on Brix's arm. "Tell me first, not her."

"I want to give her the chance to…I don't know…explain."

"Tell me, then we'll talk to her together."

"Did she say anything while you were inside the temple?"

"Not related to Dennis' death."

"Something else?"

I closed my eyes, rolled my shoulders, and raised my face to the sun when I felt its warmth. "She wants to talk to me about my father," I said, barely above a whisper.

When Brix didn't respond, I opened my eyes and turned to look at him.

"Did you hear me?"

"I did."

I put my hand on my stomach when the nausea I'd felt before returned. "Is it related?"

"It is."

I stood and held my hand out to him. "Come with me."

"Addison…"

"Please, Brix."

When he did as I asked, I led him over to where Tryst waited with my mother and Lucia. I could tell by the look in his eyes that whatever Brix knew, he did too.

"Would you mind taking my mom and Lucia back to their *casita*? Brix and I need some time."

He nodded but didn't speak.

"Addy?"

"We'll talk later, Mom." My eyes met hers, and I felt, like I did with Tryst, that there was something she knew, something she wanted to say, but I'd made up my mind. I wanted to hear it from Brix and only once we were alone.

Her eyes filled with tears. "Okay," she whispered.

Brix stood by my side, watching the golf cart drive away.

"I want to go back to our *casita*," he said once it was out of sight.

I nodded and let him lead the way. Neither of us spoke on our short walk back. With every step I took, the dread I felt multiplied. My mom knew who'd killed Dennis. I could feel it in my bones. Would she really have let me go to prison for it? I prayed that whatever Brix was about to tell me would assure me she wouldn't have.

When we stepped inside, there was a chill in the air I hadn't felt earlier. I rubbed both my arms.

"I'll light a fire," Brix offered.

I followed him into the living room, sat on the sofa, and watched him do it. When the kindling began to flame, he came over and sat beside me.

I almost told him to stop before he'd even begun. The bravado I'd felt earlier was gone. In its wake was fear.

Perhaps sensing it, Brix pulled me into his arms. He rested his head against my hair and ran his hand up and down my back.

I lost track of how much time passed. I pulled back so I could look into his eyes. "I'm ready."

I waited, watching his Adam's apple move when he swallowed.

"As you know, the name Dennis Murphy was an alias. What I learned today is that the man's real name was Brian Reagan."

My stomach lurched, and I put my hand in front of my mouth.

"Is that a name you've heard before, Addison?"

"It isn't." My eyes opened wider in horror. "Was he my father?"

"No. He was your father's half brother."

The sigh of relief I felt was short-lived, given I knew what was coming would be much worse.

"I take it you didn't know your father's first name?"

"No, I did, but it's been a long time since I've heard it."

"It's Rory."

I nodded, remembering. "That's right."

He closed his eyes and opened them slowly. "What we discovered is that up until a few days ago, your father was in prison."

My voice cracked. "For what?"

"Attempted murder in the first degree."

"Who did he try to kill?"

"Brian, but for the sake of less confusion, we can continue to refer to him as Dennis Murphy."

I leaned against the sofa, processing everything Brix had told me. "You think he's the one who killed him."

"I do."

"Is there a reason you think so? Other than the fact that he tried to kill him before?"

"The crime your father committed carries a sentence of fifteen years to life. According to the prison records Press was able to obtain, he served twenty-eight."

"I asked why you thought he was the killer, and your response was the length of time he was in prison. Why?"

"He's been up for parole several times, but it was always denied."

"Why?" I repeated.

"He refused to show remorse."

"What does that mean?"

"Your father told the parole board that if he ever got out, the first thing he'd do is finish what he started."

"Why is he out now?"

"Again, according to the reports, your father has terminal cancer. He's got six months to live, at the most."

My *father*? I'd never thought of him that way. I never would. He was no one to me. Except a murderer.

"Do you think my mother knows?"

Brix put his arm around me, pulling me so my head rested on his shoulder. "Which part?"

"Any of it? All of it?"

"I don't know."

"That's why you wanted to talk to her first."

"Yes."

"Earlier, when you said that, the first thing I thought was that my mom *knew* and she was going to let me go to prison for it. I prayed I was wrong."

"I just don't know, Addison. You said yourself she was nearly catatonic. Vader told me she couldn't remember what happened. It could be because she truly doesn't know."

"If that's the case, why did she want to talk to me about my father?"

"I can't answer that, baby."

I don't know how long we sat in silence, watching the fire. Long after it was dark. I attempted to stop my mind from racing, trying to find meaning in what Brix had told me.

"What do you want to do, Addison?" he finally asked.

"What should I do?" I really had no idea.

"We need to talk to your mom."

"Not tonight."

I felt him nod.

"What about Rory? Has he been arrested?"

"I don't think so."

"But they're looking for him?"

"Yes. Although presently, he's a person of interest, not a suspect." Brix covered his mouth when he yawned. "I don't know about you, but I could fall asleep right here."

"Go ahead."

"The bed would be a lot more comfortable, especially if you're beside me."

"After our earlier conversation, I wasn't sure you'd want me to be."

"Addison…What's your middle name?"

"Ava."

"I like it. Addison Ava Reagan, I would like nothing more than to fall asleep beside you and wake up with you in my arms not just tonight, but every night."

I looked into his eyes, waiting for him to clarify what he'd just said. He didn't. His gaze lingered on mine as if we were having a staring contest. Eventually, he cupped my cheek and smiled.

"I've been overly honest with you about my feelings. I won't ask you to tell me yours, but if there comes a time you'd like me to know, I won't mind hearing it."

I'd spent months—years even—believing Brix Avila was so far out of my league that I wasn't sure he knew I existed beyond working at his sister's wine bar and as the waitress who served his breakfast at the diner.

In only a few short days, some of the worst of my life, he'd not only admitted he had a longstanding crush on me, but now he was saying he wanted to sleep with me *every* night. What did that mean? As much as I wanted to know, I couldn't bring myself to ask.

And my feelings? God, I had no idea how I felt about anything other than I didn't know what I would have done without his support, his caring, his relentless insistence that he spend every minute he could with me. I'd be lost. I'd also be in jail for a crime I didn't commit, because I'd still believe my mother had killed Dennis—or whoever he was.

Not knowing what to say, I leaned forward and kissed him before taking his hand, standing, and leading him into the bedroom.

"I want you to know I respect what you said earlier, and while I don't think I gave you a straight answer then, I will now."

He looked hopeful. Too hopeful, and it nearly broke my heart.

"I understand it's too soon for us to have sex, Brix. You were right when you asked me if I'd be putting so much pressure on you now if I hadn't just confessed to murder. The truth is, I wouldn't. I would want to wait to see where this thing between us goes, because as much as you try to reassure me, I still have a hard time believing you could possibly feel about me the way you say you do. I'm not saying that to hurt your feelings. I'm the one with the issue. Not you."

"It isn't you, it's me?" he said from the other side of the bed. "That sounds like a breakup line."

"You know that isn't what I meant. I mean, how can we break up if we're not even together?" I regretted the words as soon as I said them, especially when his face fell. "Come on, don't look at me like that. We haven't even gone on a date, Brix."

He came around the bed and pulled me into his arms. "I plan to remedy that as soon as I'm sure it's safe for you and your mom to return to Cambria." He reached down and pulled the blanket and sheet back. "Get in bed, baby."

"Are you going to sleep in here too?"

"Only if you want me to."

"I don't think I'll be able to sleep if you don't."

"I don't think I'll be able to if I do." He winked, repeating the words almost verbatim that we'd said the first time he and I shared a bed.

27
Brix

There would be nothing easy about the day ahead, so instead of getting up, I lay in bed, holding Addison in my arms and watching her sleep.

What she'd been through in the last few days would've leveled a lesser person. The sweet, beautiful, strong, smart, resilient woman in my arms took my breath away.

I was in love with her. Head over heels. Not that Addison was ready to hear the words. Soon, though, she would be, and I wouldn't be shy about saying them.

I'd never been in love before. Not once. And now that I was, I wanted her and everyone else to know it. I'm sure anyone who knew me well, especially Tryst, already guessed it.

Watching her now made me think about my father. He'd never hidden the love he felt for my mother. Tryst had been the same way with Rosa. I finally understood why. It was as if my heart might burst with the joy of knowing she was mine. And she would be. Addison loved me as much as I loved her—there was no doubt in my mind—and in order for us to spend our lives together, we needed to determine who'd actually killed Murphy. Was his half brother, Rory, acting alone, or was Peg his accomplice? If her mother had betrayed her, my beloved Addison's heart would be broken. As much as I wanted to spare her that kind of pain, she'd asked that we speak to Peg together, and I would respect her wishes.

When I heard a knock at the front door, I picked up my phone to check the time. Who would show up here at nine in the morning? The answer was easy to figure out—my mother.

"Brix?" Addison groaned, barely opening her eyes.

"Go back to sleep, baby."

"Is someone here?"

"It's probably my mom bringing us breakfast, or something else equally ridiculous."

She rolled to her stomach and settled into the pillow. "Breakfast sounds good, but later," she mumbled before, I was sure, going right back to sleep.

"Be right there," I hollered after grabbing my jeans and closing the bedroom door behind me. Since I figured it was just my mom, I didn't bother putting a shirt on.

"Okay, hold your horses," I said when I heard another more forceful knock. I fastened the button on my pants and flung the door open. "Jeez, Ma…err…Peg."

The sight of her puffy eyes and tear-stained cheeks kept me from saying anything else other than inviting her inside.

"Is Addy still asleep?"

"Your daughter is exhausted."

She nodded. "I wanted to talk to you alone anyway."

"Peg, I can't. Addison asked that we talk to you together."

"I understand, but this is about you and her."

"First, let me grab a shirt. Then would you like some coffee?" I asked, motioning to the kitchen, admittedly curious about what she had to say.

"Please."

I eased in and out of the bedroom, threw my shirt over my head, and started a pot of coffee. I invited her to take a seat in the kitchen.

"I know you care a great deal for my daughter."

"It's more than that."

Peg nodded. "I'm afraid that getting her to trust you might not be easy."

I smiled. "I've experienced a little of that."

"That's my fault."

"Peg, you shouldn't—"

"No, Brix. It is my fault. I lied to her about her father. I've been lying to her about him all her life."

"I need to stop you before you say anything else."

"Don't stop, Mom," I heard Addison say from behind me. "I want to hear this."

I pulled out a chair for her at the table and was about to pour some coffee when she grabbed my hand.

"Don't go."

I leaned down and kissed her forehead. "I'm not going anywhere. I made coffee."

"Oh." She let go, and I smiled.

"That's what I thought."

I hurriedly poured three cups, grabbed the cream from the fridge, sugar from the cupboard, spoons from the drawer, and returned to the table.

"Go ahead, Mom," Addison said, folding her arms in front of her.

"I'm sorry, Addy."

"What for?" Her tone was clipped, but I couldn't blame her.

"I lied to you."

"I heard that part."

"Your father didn't leave us. I was the one who asked for the divorce."

"I see." Addison raised her cup to her lips, took a sip, then set it back on the table. "What else?"

"What do you mean?"

She shrugged a shoulder. "I don't know. Maybe that you knew where he was all along but didn't bother to tell me. Or that he had a half brother you also knew."

Peg looked from her daughter to me with wide eyes. "I don't know what you're talking about."

I wove my fingers with Addison's and squeezed her hand. "Let's back up for a minute."

She looked into my eyes. "Why?"

"If I may…"

"Go ahead," she muttered.

I turned to Peg. "You said you were the one who asked for the divorce. When was that?"

"Two months after Addy was born."

"She was less than a year old by the time it was final."

"That's right. I don't know—"

I held up the hand that wasn't holding Addison's. "When's the last time you saw your ex-husband?"

"The day he signed the divorce papers. I asked him to leave, and he never came back."

"Do you know where he went?"

"No idea. Rory was…distant. Increasingly so. I tried to talk to him about it many times, but it always ended in an argument followed by him walking out. I finally gave up trying. I guess there was a part of me that thought if I said I wanted a divorce, he'd talk to me, tell me what was going on in his life that he'd been refusing to share with me. Instead, he signed the paper without saying a single word."

"And left?" Addison asked.

"That's right. And, like I said, that was the last time I saw him or heard from him."

"Even when he went to prison? No one contacted you then?"

Peg looked from her daughter to me a second time. "I don't know what you're talking about."

"He went to prison, Mom, for attempted murder. Do you know who he tried to kill?"

Peg shook her head.

"His half brother, *Brian*."

Addison's mother showed absolutely no sign that she knew who that was. The look on her face remained confused. "Brian? I have no idea who that is. I never met any of his family. He said he didn't speak to them."

"No one?"

I squeezed Addison's hand again. "Peg, were you aware Rory had a half-sibling?"

She shook her head. "I just told you he refused to talk about his family."

"Did you ask?"

Peg glared at her. "Of course I asked. This conversation is veering off topic. What I came here to tell you both is that I lied about why Addy's father wasn't in our lives, and because of that, I worried you would have a hard time trusting Brix. Well, any man, but Brix is the only one who matters right now."

Addison slipped her hand from mine, took another sip of coffee, and refolded her arms after setting it down. "Why now? It just popped into your head that you should tell me the truth *today*?"

"Not exactly."

"Why, then?"

Peg sighed. "It was something Lucia and I talked about." She looked at me. "She said she'd never seen you like this with any other woman, and then she asked if I thought Addy felt the same way about you."

"Mom, leave Brix out of this," she snapped.

"Addy! I understand why you're angry with me, and I'm sorry. I just wanted you to know that things didn't happen the way I told you they did. I never should've lied to you about it."

"What else are you lying about?"

I stood and put my hand on Addison's elbow. "Peg, would you excuse us for a minute?" I looked at her daughter. "Would you come outside with me?"

Neither woman spoke, but Addison did follow me.

"What?" she barked once the front door closed behind us.

I put my hands on her shoulders. "I know you're upset, angry, hurt—all of those things—but I believe your mom is telling the truth. I don't think she knew your father went to prison, and I don't think she knows who Brian Reagan is, particularly that he's actually Dennis and your dad's half brother."

"I think you're giving her a lot of credit, Brix."

I pulled her close and wrapped my arms around her. "What we need to find out more than anything else right now is what she remembers from the night Dennis died."

Addison pulled back. "I can't help it. I'm so mad at her. She's been lying to me my whole life. I can't figure out why you think she isn't doing it now."

"Instinct, and what I want is to find out what she knows, if anything, so we can end this thing. I want the charges against you dropped, I want the real killer behind bars, and then I want to deal with the fallout of the asshole's death so we can move on with our lives."

"What fallout?"

"There's still the matter of the gambling debts."

Addison hung her head. "How are we supposed to pay them? We have nothing. Not even the diner since they burned it down."

"One step at a time. Let's finish our conversation with your mom, then figure out our next steps." We were about to head inside when David drove up in the golf cart with my mother sitting beside him.

"Why are you out here? Peg is inside, right?"

"Yes, Mama, Addison and I needed a minute."

My mom put her arm through mine and the other through Addison's. "*Mijo,* she is devastated about not telling her daughter the truth. You must show some compassion."

I stopped and turned my mother's body so she was looking at me. "We need to ask her about what happened the night of the murder. Are you sure you want to be here for this?"

My mother's eyes scrunched. *"Sí."*

Once inside, I didn't see Peg in the kitchen. Instead, I found her in the main room, standing in the center, her face raised to the sun just like Addison was yesterday.

She turned slowly and looked at the three of us.

"We're ready to continue when you are."

Peg nodded, and I motioned to the living room. "Let's sit in here instead."

I sighed with relief when Addison sat on one side of her mother while my mom sat on the other.

"Peg, I need you to try to remember everything you can about what happened the night Dennis died."

She turned toward her daughter. "But, Addy—"

"Please, Mom, whatever you remember."

Peg nodded. "It isn't much."

"That's okay. Even the most minor details can lead to clues," I said.

"How far back do you want me to go?"

"What happened at my mother's house?" I asked.

She grasped Addison's hand and closed her eyes. "Men burst in the front door. They had guns. One of them put something over my nose and mouth while the other tied my hands. I don't remember anything after that until I came to in my own living room."

"What do you remember next, Mom?"

She looked at Addison. "I opened my eyes, and I was lying on the sofa. I sat up and saw Dennis standing in the kitchen. He...he..." She covered her face with her hands. She took several deep breaths, and tears ran down her face.

"Take your time," I told her.

"I remember asking him what he was doing, why was he there. I tried to stand, but I was woozy and my head was pounding. I grabbed the back of the chair to steady myself. That's when I saw he had a gun, and it was pointed at me."

"What happened next?" gasped my mother. I shook my head at her.

"Go at your own pace, Peg."

"I heard shots. Two of them. Maybe three. I waited for the pain, knowing I was about to die, but I didn't. I must've blacked out again because when I opened my eyes, I saw the gun on the floor, not far from where

Dennis lay." She looked at Addison again. "I was so scared. I knew I had to get that gun away from him, that I couldn't let him kill me."

"He was already dead, Mom."

"I didn't know that." Peg broke down. "That's when I saw you. Oh, Addy, I'm so sorry. I never wanted to tell."

"Tell what?" she asked, but then her expression changed. "Wait. Did you think it was me who shot him?"

Peg wiped at her tears. "I just remember being so thankful that you saved my life. Nothing after that. Did I pass out again? The next thing I knew, we were at the police station, sitting in a room, and Conrad was kneeling in front of me."

Addison held both of Peg's hands. "Mom, I didn't kill him. When I came in through the back door, you were standing over him with the gun in your hand. I took it from you, and then I did think you were about to pass out, so I helped you into the chair. Right after that, Vader arrived."

"Wait." My mother stood and looked out the window. "David is coming back, and there's someone with him."

"Uncle Tryst?"

She shook her head, and her eyes opened wide. "It's the sheriff."

While my mother looked horrified, I hoped this meant he came with news about the investigation, maybe even that they'd found Rory.

"Be right back," I said, hurrying out to meet him.

"Vader, this is a surprise."

"It's over, Brix. Rory Reagan turned up in San Luis Obispo General, barely alive. I think killing his half brother was all he was hanging on for. He confessed to killing him in detail matching the crime scene. There's more. The bullets we recovered, one from the kitchen and the other from inside the victim, don't match the gun with Peg's and Addy's prints on it. The third set of fingerprints matched Brian's, so my guess is the gun belonged to him. Speaking of that gun, we found another bullet lodged in the wall near the front door. I think Reagan…err…Brian, got a shot off at the same time Rory did. He just missed."

That explained a great deal, particularly why both Addison and her mother had traces of gun residue on their hands.

"Why are you here, Sheriff?"

"Conrad."

"I see. She's inside if you want to talk to her."

"Peg?"

I smiled. "Yeah, *Conrad,* Peg."

Addison was standing in the doorway when I turned to go in.

"Did you hear all that?" I asked when we both stepped aside to let Vader go past us.

"I did."

"He confessed, but more importantly, it sounds as though the evidence supports him being the killer."

She stepped forward, and I took her in my arms. "Is it really over?"

It wasn't. As I'd said earlier, there was still the matter of the debt Murphy owed the Killeens. I wouldn't remind her of that now, though.

We went inside and found Peg in Vader's arms. My mother stood near them, smiling while tears ran down her face. She held her hand out to me.

"Oh, *Mijo,* I am so happy it is over."

I wanted to be as happy as she was, but until I could settle Murphy's debt, I still feared for both Addison's and her mother's lives.

My cell rang, and I groaned when I saw it was my sister calling. "Hey, Alex."

"Is it true? Maddox said he heard they caught the real killer."

I briefly wondered how my brother-in-law heard about it, but quickly realized there wasn't much related to law enforcement—or espionage—his father didn't know before the rest of us. "It is true."

"That means the Wicked Winemakers' Ball can be held as planned."

I rolled my eyes at my sister's one-track mind. However, this did present the perfect opportunity to tell her about my plan.

"Be right back," I told Addison. She nodded but then grabbed my free hand and pulled me closer to kiss me.

"What was that?"

"Nothing. Listen, there's something I want to talk to you about relating to the bachelor auction."

"Brix, I swear, if you're about to renege—"

"It isn't anything like that. However, things have to be done my way or I will."

"You're such a jerk."

"You won't think so once you've heard my plan."

When I went inside, Peg, Vader, and my mom were seated on the sofa. Addison was on the floor near the fireplace Vader must've lit.

All four turned and looked at me.

"My mom has questions. I thought we should wait for you." I sat down next to Addison and leaned up against the wall.

"About?"

"Who is Brian Reagan?"

I looked at Vader, wondering why he hadn't filled her in. When he didn't look back at me, I cleared my throat. "We explained to you before that Dennis Murphy was an alias and that he went by another, Patrick Sullivan."

Peg nodded. "I remember."

"At the time, we weren't able to determine his real identity."

Peg's eyes opened wide, and she turned pale. "He's Rory's *brother*?"

"Half brother, but yes."

She turned to Addison. "You thought I knew."

"I wasn't sure what to think, Mom, especially when you said you lied to me about my father leaving us."

"I had no idea. I swear."

"There's more in the prison reports Press was able to get his hands on," said Vader, not even attempting to hide his irritation that once again our "vigilante group" was able to get information he hadn't been.

"It seems that shortly before each of his parole hearings, Rory would receive anonymous letters. I read a couple that were in the digital file, and I have no doubt they were from Brian."

"What did they say?"

"Murphy would get him all fired up right before the parole hearing, knowing Rory wouldn't be able to hold it together."

"What else did it say, Vader?" asked Addison.

"I don't recall the exact words."

"What do you recall, then?" She was clearly pissed.

"There were threats."

"Do you think Dennis knew I was Rory's ex-wife and Addison was his daughter?" asked Peg.

"I don't have any doubt that he did. One I read said he'd located the two of you."

"You said he was in prison for attempting to kill him. Do you know why?"

"Not yet, but I've got my team working on it." Vader looked at me. "As I'm sure you do too."

28

Addison

As much as I was anxious to get home, a part of me was sad about leaving Tryst's ranch so soon. I felt such peace while I was here, even though when I arrived, my life couldn't have looked grimmer.

I looked out the window of the plane as we took off, hoping one day I could return. Brix raised my hand to his lips.

"What are you thinking about?" he asked.

"What a wonderful place this is."

"I couldn't agree more. I wish I could spend more time here. Actually, that isn't what I wish at all."

I scrunched my eyes. "What do you mean?"

"I don't wish it just for me, Addison. I want to spend more time here, and when I do, I want you to be with me."

I smiled. "I'd really like that."

"Yeah?" His expression was so hopeful, which surprised me as much as his laughter did a few days ago.

"Do you really doubt I'd want to?"

"Last night, you said we hadn't even gone out on a date yet."

"Yeah, about that…"

He raised his eyebrows.

"I want you to know I wasn't suggesting you had to take me out somewhere."

"Oh, but I'm going to. Just you wait and see."

When I leaned over and kissed his cheek, Brix turned his face, and our lips met instead.

"You know the ball is this weekend."

Actually, it was the furthest thing from my mind. "I really don't think I'm up for it. I'm sure Alex will understand."

"She might, but I won't. We had an agreement, remember? You have to be the winning bidder."

I couldn't tell if he was serious or teasing me. "Since it's your money anyway, why don't you just bid on yourself?"

He shook his head. "Not a chance. Our first date depends on you honoring your agreement."

"Brix, you better be joking."

He shook his head and winked at me. "If you think I'm bad, wait until Alex hears you aren't willing to bid."

29

Brix

We'd been in the air for about an hour when my phone buzzed with a message from Ridge, asking me to contact him as soon as I could.

Not wanting to wake her, I eased Addison's arm from around me. She shifted without opening her eyes.

When I stood and went to the back of the plane, Vader followed.

"Did you get a message from Ridge too?" he asked.

"Sure did." I opened the door to the plane's rear stateroom, we went inside, and I closed it behind us.

"Hey, Brix," he said, answering my call.

"Ridge, I've got Vader here with me."

"Listen, this new prosecutor is becoming a huge pain in the ass. She's insisting on talking to both Addy and her mom."

"Why? They're in the clear."

"Evidently, it's about something else. Anyway, she's demanding I tell her where they are."

"Why you? Why isn't she contacting Zin?"

"I guess I'm the only one who answers my phone."

"Stop answering it."

"I'll get in touch with her," said Vader. "She should be working with me, not around me."

"Her name is Seraphina—"

"Yeah, Ridge, I know." Vader rolled his eyes.

"What about Reilly?"

"It's amazing what the man will agree to tell us if he thinks we're going to supply him with his next hit."

Vader's eyes scrunched. "Tell me you're not."

"Fuck, no," snapped Ridge. "What do you take us for? Don't answer that. Anyway, Bones is here now."

"Bones" was Ridge's younger brother, Dalton. Like my sibling Cristobal, he was a doctor. He practiced traditional medicine while Cris specialized in genetics. Ridge bringing Bones in was smart. He'd be able to monitor Reilly's withdrawals, although I doubted they were in full force yet.

"What's he willing to give up?" I asked.

"The better question is who. It seems everyone in FAIM is fair game. Killeens too."

"What does he know about them?"

"To begin with, as you're aware, they're known primarily for racketeering; however, according to Reilly, they've been working with FAIM for several months, trying to expand meth distribution on the West Coast."

"That's why they wouldn't go after the bounty we offered on Murphy. It wasn't because they were afraid of the fallout."

"Makes sense."

"Can you get a feel for whether the Killeens will go after Peg for the money Murphy owed them?" I asked.

"Murphy?"

"Fuck, Ridge, you know who I mean."

"Sorry," he muttered. "Gets confusing. Anyway, whether Reilly thinks they will or not, we're amassing plenty to bargain with, Brix. Hey, Vader, I have no doubt that when his withdrawals get worse, you're gonna want to read him his rights."

"I'll send one of the deputies. Where are you holding him?"

I heard Ridge snicker and almost laughed myself. "Where do you think?"

"I hope to hell we never have reason to search the Los Cab wine caves, and if we do, I hope you and your ancestors have been smart enough to clear out all the dead bodies."

I didn't bother to inform Vader that wasn't where they were. He'd know soon enough after our plane landed. "No idea what he's talking about. Do you, Ridge?"

He laughed. "None whatsoever. Looks like the interrogation is underway again. I better get back in there. When will you be back?"

"About an hour. Maybe less."

"Glad to hear it. I thought you might stay another week or two. I would've if I were you."

"Time you scheduled a visit, my friend. I'm sure Tryst would welcome you gladly. I might've been tempted to stay if Alex hadn't called to say the ball is back on for this weekend."

"Shit," he muttered. "Really? I kind of forgot all about it."

"You better not let Alex hear that."

"Since I only said it to the two of you, if she does get wind, I'll know who to exact my revenge on."

"See ya, Ridge. Hey, wait. Are Zin or Cru with you?"

"Negative. They're both off, taking care of some other business. I'm not sure what Zin is doing, but

Cru is in the winery. We thought that would be safest, given he and Kick would much rather kill Reilly than let him talk."

"Roger that. See you soon."

"You should go back to your seat," I said to Vader once the call with Ridge ended. He got my message and left.

The first person I called was Zin. When he didn't pick up, I left a message telling him about the meeting and asking him to get in touch with either Ridge or me as soon as possible.

"Hey, Brix, I heard there's good news," said Cru when I called him next.

Fuck, was it all over the valley already? "Where'd you hear it from?"

He laughed. "Burns Butler was here a little while ago. Said that since you were all headed back from Mexico, there were a few more things he wanted to set up, mainly over at your place."

My guess was Tryst, who'd stayed behind, alerted Burns that we were on our way. "Sounds good. Listen, there's something I need your help with, but first, tell me how crush is going."

"Picked the last of the late-harvest Zinfandel yesterday. Everything else is either in barrels or vats."

While my first inclination was to ask whether Maddox and Naughton had helped get it all done, I thanked him.

"Hope I didn't overstep."

"Not at all. I told you the last time we talked that I wanted you to take over more of the main label winemaking; nothing like jumping right into the deep end."

"What do you need help with, or was that it?"

"I want you to stay abreast of how Reilly's questioning is going. If you think we have enough to make a deal, I want you to set up a meeting with James Dunn, head of the Killeen organization."

"You sure about me being involved? Isn't Ridge your go-to guy?"

I had a lot of work to do with my younger brother, and I would start today. "You're the only one I want to do it. I also want you there as my second."

"You got it. When and where?"

"As soon as you think we have enough to arrange it. Neutral location, but public."

"How about the speakeasy behind Pappy's?"

"Perfect. Thanks, Cru."

I'd lied to my brother when I said he was the only one I wanted to contact Dunn, and I was ashamed I had. He was actually my fifth choice if I counted Zin as an option. From now on, I needed to remember to put him first. Especially since he hadn't needed to ask the purpose of the meeting.

When I returned to my seat next to Addison, she was awake.

"Is everything okay?" she asked.

"Getting there." My brother saying Burns was at Los Cab made me realize I hadn't talked to her about where she'd be staying once we landed at Seahorse. If she wasn't comfortable staying with me, there would be my next choice. It might be the best idea anyway since there would be room for Peg too if she didn't feel comfortable staying at my mom's place again.

Addison nudged me. "Brix?"

"Sorry, thinking about logistics."

"Time to get back to your life," she said quietly enough that it was almost a whisper.

"*Our* lives."

"You're right. I worry about what my mom will do. She's definitely going to have to look for a job even if the insurance pays the claim on the diner. I'm sure Alex is anxious for me to get back to work too."

I leaned over and kissed her. "That isn't what I meant. I'm thinking more about where you're going to sleep tonight."

Her eyes scrunched, and she looked like she wanted to say something but was holding back.

"I hate to bring up anything unpleasant, but there are still a couple of things that need to be resolved."

"The money," she mumbled, turning her head to look out the window.

"I want you to know I'm going to take care of it."

Her head spun back around. "What does *that* mean?"

I scrubbed my face with my hand, cursing myself for bringing it up. "It'll be taken care of," I repeated.

She looked across the aisle at her mom, who glanced over her shoulder at us.

"You can't," she whispered. "This isn't your responsibility."

"It isn't yours either."

I was surprised when her eyes filled with tears. "I can't let you. You've done too much already."

Afraid this discussion would escalate into an argument, I got up. "Let's talk somewhere else."

"Where?"

"We'll have privacy in here." I opened the door to the stateroom where Vader and I had been a few minutes ago.

"Um, wow," she said, eyeing the bed and making me realize I should've brought her in here much earlier. When her heated gaze met mine, I closed the door, then trapped her up against it.

I desperately wanted to kiss every inch of her, but there were things I needed to say first.

"I haven't done *too much*. It could never be too much."

"Brix—"

"I need to finish, Addison. Everything to do with your life is part of my life too. I meant it when I said I want to fall asleep beside you and wake up with you in my arms every day for the rest of my life. In order to get you to even consider whether you want that too, every threat, every danger, every worry you have has to be taken care of. You say it isn't my responsibility, but you're wrong. It isn't anyone's responsibility *but* mine."

"You didn't say the rest of your life."

"Wait. What? Yeah, I did."

"You said every night."

"*For the rest of my life.* God, Addison, don't you have any idea how much I love you?"

"You love me?"

I rested my forehead against hers. "Are you saying you really didn't know?"

"Not the love part."

"Well, I do. How does that make you feel? Because the last thing I want is for you to think I'm pressuring you—"

She put her fingertip on my lips. "First you never talk, then it's all you do."

When she pressed her tongue against my lips, I opened to her. When she turned us around so my back was to the door, I followed her lead. She angled her head to deepen our kiss, and I let her. No one had ever kissed me the way she was. Maybe kissed me back, but not initiated it, and I'd never been as turned on. But a plane wasn't a tree house.

She pulled back and covered my mouth with her hand. "I need to talk now."

I nodded.

"Can we do it there?" She moved her hand from my mouth and pointed to the bed.

"Um, sure."

She lay down first and pulled me next to her.

"I like this side of you."

"You sure about that?"

"I was raised by a strong woman, and I have one as a sister. So yeah, I like it."

"This is the part where you let me talk."

I put my finger against my own lips and nodded.

"I'm going to be honest with you, Brix; I'm not ready to talk about my feelings."

It was damn hard to keep my mouth shut, but I did.

"I can tell you I care about you in a way I never have for anyone else. I guess the only thing stopping me from allowing myself to just go along with all these crazy things you say, is my fear that you'll change your mind about me."

"Never," I whispered, unable to hold it in.

"If we spent every night together, where would we be?"

"Wherever you want."

She smirked. "My place? Seriously?"

"I may have to buy you a bigger bed."

She laughed, but then her expression changed. "Are you going to pay them off?"

"If that's what it takes."

"I wish there were another solution."

"Me too, but I think it's the only thing that will work."

My cell rang, and as much as I didn't want to answer it, by the ringtone, I knew it was Zin. "I need to take this, baby."

"Hey, Brix, I saw I missed your call. I'd say I'm sorry, but once you hear what I was doing instead, you'll understand why I didn't."

"Go ahead."

"I contacted the FBI to open dialogue on what we're learning from Reilly. Turns out, they're way ahead of us."

Zin had a cousin with the bureau. No doubt that's what he meant about opening dialogue with them. "What's that mean?"

"With or without his information, they're getting ready to launch a full-blown sting operation."

"Jesus, Zin, this is *not* something you should know."

"Yeah, whatever. Anyway, I predict that very soon, neither the Killeens nor FAIM will be much of a threat. From what my contact said, this will literally be the biggest shutdown of a narcotics operation in FBI history."

I was glad both Addison and I were sitting down on the bed. This news was staggering. "Hey, when you get a chance, Ridge is having trouble with a prosecutor who's pressuring him about Addison's and Peg's whereabouts."

"Damn, is she still buzzing around? Look, her case has gone to shit since the man she was prosecuting is dead. Anyway, I'll quash this meeting. The fucking district attorney, man. He knows I represent Addison. What the hell is he thinking?" Zin must've ended the call since I heard the chimes indicating it.

I had no idea what investigation he was talking about, but it had to involve Murphy.

"Do you really think it'll be over soon?" Addison asked.

"I hope so. I can tell you this, if Zin is right about what's about to go down, they sure as hell won't risk another extortion charge trying to collect a couple hundred grand."

"We need to tell my mom."

"We will, but there's something I need to talk to you about first."

"Brix—"

"Come on, baby, just hear me out."

She folded her arms but nodded.

"There are three nights until the Wicked Winemakers' Ball and the auction. As I said earlier, I want to spend every one of them with you." She took a breath to speak, and I silenced her with a quick kiss. "I want you to trust I have a very good reason for saying this, but I want us to wait to make love until the night of the ball."

Her eyes scrunched. "A *very* good reason?"

"A very, *very* good reason."

"Okay."

"Okay, but we'll still be together, right?"

"As if I could get away from you if I wanted to. And, Brix, I don't want to."

There was a knock at the door, and I heard my mother's voice. "*Mi-jo, Ad-dy,* time to get out of bed. Press says he wants to land the plane."

"Sorry, baby, I was hoping she'd stay asleep until after we landed."

"I heard you, and you're in *trou-ble*." My mom's laughter faded as she walked away.

30

Addison

As promised, Brix and I spent every night together and at his place since my mother assured me she was perfectly capable of staying *alone*. Not that I believed that's what she was doing, especially after Brix and I had gone to my apartment to pack up the rest of my clothes and the neighbor asked why the sheriff had been at the house the last two nights.

We hadn't heard anything about the sting Zin told us about, but he hadn't given any indication when it might happen, so it could be months before we did.

Connor Reilly had been arrested along with the five other men who participated in my mother's abduction and what happened to Lucia and Trevino.

Brix reported Reilly had confirmed Murphy offered them a share of the life insurance payout once my mother was dead, and that it had been his job to sabotage the security systems at Los Cab while two of the other guys delivered my mother to her house where Dennis was waiting.

While I'd tried to get out of going to the ball, neither Brix nor Alex would let me. Earlier today, she'd called and insisted that Sam and I come to her place to get ready. When I told her I didn't plan to dress any differently than any other year when I was working behind the scenes, her only response was, "We'll see about that."

Still, I packed the black pants and tuxedo shirt I wore at Stave for special-occasion events and accepted Brix's offer of driving me to the vineyard estate where Alex and her husband lived.

After we spent five minutes in the car, kissing goodbye, Alex rapped on the window. "Damn, Brix, you'll see her in a couple of hours. Let her go."

I kissed him two more times and followed Alex inside. "Where's Coco?" I asked when I didn't see the baby.

"With Sam's mom. She was the only babysitter we could find tonight."

Sam came out from around the corner. "Hey, girlfriend. Asking about the baby and not me? I guess that's how it is now that she's going to be your niece."

I hugged her hard. "Stop that. Brix and I aren't getting married."

"Yet," both she and Alex said at the same time.

"Come on," said Alex, grabbing my hand and pulling me toward the stairs. "You need to try on your gown."

I stopped mid-stair. "Wait. No. I told you I was wearing what I always do." I felt my eyes fill with tears. I didn't know whose gown it was that she wanted me to try on, but I knew for sure it wouldn't fit me.

Alex turned around and put her hands on my shoulders. "Addison Reagan, have I ever done anything to intentionally hurt you? And would I ever allow it if I knew that's what someone was doing?"

"No," I answered in a tiny voice.

"Then, *trust* me."

"You sound just like your brother," I mumbled as I followed her the rest of the way up.

She looked over her shoulder and winked. "I'll take that as the compliment I know you meant it to be."

When she opened a bedroom door, I saw her mother, my mother, and Sorcha Butler waiting.

"Here she is," said Sorcha in her thick Scottish accent. "You must hurry and try the gown on in case I need to make any alterations." She motioned to a screen. Behind it hung the most beautiful dress I'd ever seen. It was a deep shade of green and made of satin covered with the same-color sheer fabric. It had a draped bodice that flowed into the loose waist, bloused sleeves, and a sweeping skirt.

I bit my bottom lip, took off my sweater and jeans, and slipped the dress over my head. It cascaded down my body like it was made for me.

I stared at myself in the mirror until I could no longer see through my tears. "It's perfect," I whispered.

"Let me see," said Sorcha, taking my hand and pulling me out from behind the partition.

"You look so beautiful," gasped my mother.

"She's an angel," said Lucia.

"Sam," I heard Alex call out from the doorway. "Get up here. Wait until you see our princess."

When my best friend rushed in, she gasped like my mom had. "Oh, wow." She handed me the bag she was carrying. "Put these on underneath, and I swear that man will be on his knees the minute he sees you tonight."

"What's in here?"

"A gift from Brix, which is how he'll know you're wearing it."

Sorcha circled me a couple of times, checking the fit of the gown. "Nothing for me to do besides get dressed myself," she said.

"I told you it would be perfect," Lucia said, following her out of the room. "I don't know why you doubted me."

"I guess I best get dressed too," said my mom, kissing my forehead.

"You're going tonight too?"

"Oh, yes, and wait until you see how handsome my date looks in his tuxedo." She winked and went in the same direction Sorcha and Lucia had.

"Us too, girlfriend," said Alex, grabbing Sam's arm. "We'll be back in a few minutes to help with hair and makeup."

"I feel like Cinderella," I whispered to Sam when we were on our way out the front door of Alex's house, where a limousine waited to take us to the ball.

"I can guarantee you're going to *love* where you are when the clock strikes midnight."

"Alex!" scolded Sam.

"Don't worry. I'm not going to say anything more."

Part of me wanted to pry it out of my best friend, but another part of me didn't want to know until I was in Brix's arms.

"You look so beautiful," said Sam as I took the hand of the driver, who helped me in the car.

"She cleans up good," said Alex, squeezing my hand. "I'm so proud of you, Addy. Not because of what you're wearing. I mean, you always look beautiful. And if you don't believe me, my brother will assure you I'm right." She smiled, and her eyes filled with tears. "I'm proud of you because no one could've gone through everything you did with the same amount of grace."

I wanted to argue that I wasn't graceful at all, but instead, I thanked her.

"We're all set," Alex said to the driver, who closed the door.

"What about my mom? And yours? And Sorcha?"

"They have a driver of their own tonight."

Only after we arrived and Alex and Sam took off in different directions, did I realize I'd never said anything to them about how beautiful they looked too. "I'm such a dolt," I mumbled.

"You are nothing of the kind. You are enchanting."

I turned around at the sound of Tryst's voice. "You're here. I'm so glad."

"My niece would never let me hear the end of it if I wasn't at the Wicked Winemakers' Ball." He held out his arm. "May I escort you to your table?"

When I'd said I felt like Cinderella earlier, I really meant it. I'd never felt more like a princess than I did tonight.

When we arrived at the table, Brix was in a conversation with Ridge. When his friend pointed, he stood and walked toward us. "May I?" he asked his uncle.

Tryst kissed the back of my hand, and Brix took it in his.

"You take my breath away, Miss Reagan."

"You've always taken mine away, Mister Avila."

While his tuxedo was black, his pocket square was the same color as my dress. When I looked closer, I realized it was actually the same fabric.

"Would you like a glass of wine and perhaps to look at the silent auction items?"

This was the first time I didn't know what they were ahead of time since it was usually my job to get the bid sheets set up. "I'd love both. Thank you."

"Allow me." Ridge picked up a bottle from the table and poured two glasses.

"Keep this up, and you'll be able to take over my job at the wine bar." I winked at Brix, whose face broke out in an ear-to-ear smile.

"I saw a few items I thought we might like to bid on," he said, leading me over to the auction tables.

I took a sip of my wine and clung to Brix's arm.

"There isn't a person in this room who hasn't noticed your beauty, Addison."

"They're probably wondering what I'm doing out here instead of behind the scenes."

"Brix, what a nice surprise to see your name on the list of bachelors," said a woman I recognized from previous years but couldn't recall her name.

"Heidi, you remember Addison Reagan?"

She looked me up and down. "I'm not sure I do."

"It was nice to meet you," I said behind me when Brix whisked me away, telling the woman to have a nice night.

"I was polite only on your account. I don't typically engage in small talk," he whispered, leaning into me.

"You don't say?"

I lost track of how many auction sheets Brix added his name and bid amount to. "Alex will love that you're driving the bids up so high," I commented when I saw the amount he wrote on a four-day weekend in Laguna Beach.

"I bid that much because I want to win," he said, stroking his finger down the side of my face.

When we got to the end of the row of tables, Brix pulled me around the corner and gathered me in his arms. "I wish we could begin our date right now. I don't want to wait any longer."

"I wish we could too."

"Tell me, Addison. Are you wearing the gifts I sent for you?"

"You'll have to wait and see." When I tried to walk away, he wrapped his arm around my waist and pulled me against him.

"Can you feel how much I want you, baby?"

"I feel dizzy," I said, leaning my back against his front. "Maybe I'm coming down with something. I think we *should* leave."

"I'll never speak to either of you again," said Alex, walking up behind us. She pinched Brix's arm. "I agreed to your terms, brother. You are the last bachelor in the auction tonight, and you will stay until I declare your *anonymous bidder* the winner."

"And not a minute longer," he said, leading me back in the direction of our table.

"There's my mom and Vader." I pointed to the bar. "Would you mind if we said hello?"

Ten minutes and several interruptions later from people who wanted to talk to Brix, we finally made our way over.

I kissed my mother's cheek. "You look gorgeous in that dress," I whispered. The pale-pink lace gown looked like it was custom-made for her.

"Thank you. Lucia picked it out."

I noticed Brix and Vader head-to-head in conversation. "He detests small talk with people from the wine industry, yet it will be hard for me to pull him away from the sheriff."

"Conrad?"

"Excuse me, Brix. Yes, Peg?"

"I believe they're about to serve dinner."

"Thanks, Mom," I said as he escorted her away.

Brix held out his arm. "Shall we?"

"Tsk, tsk, Brix. I thought the point of the bachelor auction was that you weren't supposed to arrive with a date," said another woman I recognized but couldn't recall her name. "I hope she doesn't mind finding her own way home tonight."

"You could never afford me, Isabel."

"That was Isabel Van Orr?" I gasped as he led me away.

"Indeed, it was."

"Her father is Baron Van Orr. They're, well, she could easily afford to bid on you, Brix."

"But she could never win, Addison. I don't care if it costs me a million dollars. You are the only woman I'm leaving with tonight or any other night."

By the time dinner was over and the silent auction item winners announced—Brix won all he bid on—I had a death grip on the napkin in my lap.

"Is everything okay?" he asked, attempting to pry it out of my hand.

"I've never been more uncomfortable," I said, looking over my shoulder at the groups of women gathered together, talking, none of whom tried to hide the fact that I was the subject of their conversations.

"Ignore them," Brix said without taking his eyes off me. "Not a single one matters to me. Only you do."

"I told Sam earlier that I felt like Cinderella. I do more now. It's like most of the women here are my evil stepsisters."

He laughed. "It's almost over. Alex just texted that the bachelors are supposed to report backstage." When he kissed me and pushed his chair back, I did too.

"I can't stay out here," I said when he raised a brow.

Suddenly, Tryst was beside me. "May I have this dance, Addy?"

I hadn't even noticed the number of couples out on the floor. I turned to Brix, who leaned closer.

"You are the most stunning woman in this room tonight, baby. Don't run off and hide. Be as proud of yourself as I am of you."

"I couldn't have said it better myself," Tryst said once we were dancing. "If my nephew hadn't swept you off your feet, I'm sure there are many men in the room who would've liked the chance to."

"Thank you, but—"

"Shh, now. Let the music drown all the negative thoughts from your mind."

Tryst and I danced until I heard Alex ask everyone to take their seats for the evening's big event.

One by one, the bachelors went up for bid, starting with two winemaker brothers who weren't in Brix's circle of friends. When the bidding started for the first, Tryst's demeanor changed from affable to surly. It continued with the second. When neither of their bids reached more than a thousand dollars, Tryst appeared happy again.

"I don't recognize either one of them," I said when everyone clapped.

"You are better for it."

When the next bachelor—Kick—took the stage, the crowd became more animated and remained lively through the six who followed. Snapper, Zin, Cru, Press, Beau, and Ridge each had winning bids between five and ten thousand dollars. Ridge's was the highest.

"May I present our final bachelor of the evening, Brix Avila." There was a long burst of applause. "Now, ladies, I know you've been saving your pennies—okay, hundred-dollar bills—waiting for the day I'd finally talk my brother into being in the auction."

My eyes met Brix's, and I nearly laughed when I saw he looked more uncomfortable than I had most of the night.

"Given the magnitude of this development, we have a phone-in bidder. Sam will be bidding on her behalf. Let's get started. Who would like to place the opening bid?"

"Ten thousand dollars!" shouted Heidi, who had given me the once-over earlier in the night.

When Isabel bid fifteen thousand, I put my hand over my mouth to cover my laugh.

"Twenty thousand," said Sam, raising her paddle.

"Twenty-five thousand," said a woman from the back of the room.

Sam raised her paddle again. "Thirty."

I glanced at Brix to see if he was giving her the stink eye for raising it by so much, but instead, he was smiling.

"Thirty thousand for a date with my big brother!" Alex pretended to wipe her brow. She turned to him. "And, ladies, this is all with him keeping the details of the date secret! Do you all know something I don't?"

"Forty thousand," shouted Isabel.

"Fifty," came from a different woman in the back of the room.

"This is ridiculous," I heard Heidi say. "He's hot, but no one is *that* hot."

Alex turned to Sam. "Fifty thousand going once…"

I saw Brix's hand flex and realized that he was giving her signals.

"Sixty thousand," Sam countered.

"Seventy!" I recognized Isabel's voice. Had Brix realized what he was doing when he challenged her by saying she could never afford him? I watched his hand, and he tucked in three fingers.

Sam shook her head and laughed. "Eighty!"

"Eighty thousand going once, going twice…"

"One hundred thousand." The excitement was gone from Isabel's voice. Now she sounded angry.

Sam nodded and raised her paddle. "One fifty."

Isabel got up from her table and stalked out of the room.

"One hundred fifty thousand going once...twice... sold to our anonymous bidder! Congratulations, whoever you are. I hope you *really* enjoy this date!"

"Come with me," said Tryst, taking my hand and pulling me up from the table.

"Wait!" I yelped, reaching down for my purse.

"We must hurry!" said Tryst, leading me out of the winery and over to a waiting SUV.

He opened the back door and helped me inside. Alex's husband was in the driver's seat.

"Hi, Maddox."

He whistled. "*Wowzer*, Addy. Brix is a lucky man."

"Have a magical time!" said Tryst, closing my door. As soon as he had, Maddox stepped on the gas.

"Where is Brix?"

"If our timing is right, he should be waiting at the rendezvous point." He chuckled. "I always wanted to say that. *Rendezvous*."

I rested against the seat and closed my eyes.

"Alex said the bid got up to a hundred and fifty grand. She's yankin' my chain, right?"

"Nope. Brix paid that much money for a date with himself," I said under my breath.

"No, sister. Brix paid it for a date with you. He would've paid twice that. Five times that."

I smirked at his reflection in the rearview. "Knock it off, Maddox."

His expression changed. "It's true, Addy. Hey, there they are. Right on time."

I looked at where he was pointing. Brix was standing next to a helicopter, but when we pulled up, he strode over to my door.

When he opened it and held out his hand, it felt like the air swirling around us changed, and it had nothing to do with the helicopter's blades.

"Addison," he murmured, pulling me into his arms and spinning us around. "Are you ready for our date?"

"I'm ready for it all, Brix."

31

Brix

I draped my jacket over Addison's shoulders when I saw her shiver, and fastened her into the seat beside me, then handed her a headset.

Her eyes were bright. She was excited, but I loved that she didn't ask where we were going. I almost couldn't believe I was finally and actually going to be able to *surprise* her with her fantasy.

"All set," I said to Naughton, who had not just agreed to fly us up to Big Sur, but volunteered when he heard I planned to drive up after the ball.

Earlier in the day, Ridge drove my car and our bags up, and Press drove him back. I had damn good friends.

Naughton took us out over the ocean, fully illuminated by tonight's full moon.

"Flight time is about twenty minutes," Naughton said.

Addison's eyes met mine, but she still didn't ask.

"I love you," I mouthed.

She smiled, and I watched as she took in everything below us. It seemed only minutes later Naughton turned toward the shoreline.

Addison gasped. "Brix? How did you know?"

"Just the first of many fantasies I plan to make come true for you, baby."

"But…how?"

"Remember I told you I sometimes eavesdropped on your conversations with Sam? This was one of them."

Her eyes filled with tears, and she brought my hand to her lips. "Thank you," she murmured.

Naughton brought the chopper down on the helipad where another SUV was waiting for us.

"Welcome, Miss Reagan and Mr. Avila," the man said after Naughton helped us both out.

"Thanks, man," I said, patting him on the back before he got back in. "I owe you."

Naughton shook his head. "It's what friends do, Brix."

"You must be freezing," Addison said as we hurried over to the SUV.

"I doubt I'll ever feel cold again."

"Is this your first time at the inn?" the driver asked.

He welcomed us and ran down the list of amenities when we told him it was. I didn't bother listening. I had everything planned out, all designed to make Addison's dream come true.

We'd spend three nights in our tree house, making love for hours, talking, having our meals brought to us, and of course, I'd scheduled a couple's massage. Outside of that, no matter what Addison wanted to do, I'd go along happily.

"This is the best date, no, the best night of my life, Brix. I can't believe you did this for me." She put her arm through mine and rested her head on my shoulder. "Please, God, if this is a dream, don't ever wake me up."

I kissed her forehead. "I feel the same way."

"You won't be able to see much tonight, but tomorrow the views will astound you."

Addison looked up at me. "Thank you for this."

"The pleasure is mine, my love."

"Everything has been delivered to your tree house," the man said when he pulled up near the stairs. "If there's anything else you need, just call the front desk, and we'll bring it right over. I'll show you the way up, give you a quick tour, and be on my way."

"We're good," I told him, handing him a hundred-dollar bill.

"Thank you, sir, and here's the key."

I handed it to Addison before scooping her into my arms.

She giggled. "What are you doing?"

"There is no way I'm going to risk you getting hurt before our date begins."

"I don't want you to get hurt either, Brix. As for our date, I feel like it started in our *casita* on Tryst's ranch and is still going."

When we got to the top of the stairs, Addison put the key into the door, and when it opened, I carried her inside. "If you'll let me, I'll keep our date going for the rest of our lives."

"You mean that, don't you?"

"With all my heart." I led her from the entryway into the main part of the tree house. There was a light on by the bed, but since the fireplace was lit, I turned it off. "Look up there." I pointed to the skylight over the bed. "Someone told me there's no better place for stargazing than right here."

"Do you really want to look at the stars, Brix?"

I put my arms around her waist. "No, baby, I only want to see you. All of you. I want to touch you and taste you and sink so deep into your body that we become one."

"What are you waiting for?" Addison turned around, and I lowered her zipper. When she faced me, she put one finger in the center of my chest and gave me a push.

I landed on my butt on the end of the bed and watched in awe as she shimmied out of the dress she'd looked so beautiful in. Her body beneath it, though, made me dizzy with desire. "Come closer, baby, but leave the bra and panties on."

Two steps, and she was standing between my legs.

"I want to touch you." I ran my hands over the naked parts of her and the gold lace of the lingerie I'd given her. "How did you feel wearing this for me, Addison?"

She put her hands on my shoulders. "So sexy."

When I leaned forward and tongued her nipple through the lace, she wove her fingers in my hair. "You like having my mouth on you, don't you, my darling?"

"I love it, Brix."

I moved to her other nipple before unclasping her bra and letting it fall to the floor. I licked. I bit. I sucked its perfection, then lay back on the bed and grasped Addison's perfect ass.

"Climb up on me, baby. Right here." I showed her where I wanted her to put her knees, so she straddled me.

"Brix, I—"

"I can't wait to feel you rubbing yourself against me."

Her eyes flared, and she flushed with desire. Once she was above me, I rose up so I could ravish her mouth in the same way I did her breast, kissing, nipping, sucking her lips and tongue. The deeper I went, the harder she ground her pussy against my cock that strained against my pants.

I didn't want to rush this; I wanted to savor every second of the first time I made love to Addison Reagan. She'd been the woman of my fantasies for longer than I could remember, which meant I had an endless list of things I wanted to do to her and have her do to me.

"God, I love your curves," I told her when I put my hands on her waist and she closed her scrunched eyes.

I rolled us both so she was on her back, then shifted off the bed. "I need these off. I've been dreaming about tasting that perfect pussy for the second time." I eased her panties over her bottom while I kissed her abdomen and down a straight line to her pussy, tossing the gold lace, wet from her arousal, over my shoulder.

"Brix, please," she begged.

"What, baby?"

"I want to see you. Let me look at you."

I pulled the bow tie I'd loosened earlier from around my neck, removed my cuff links, and unfastened my tuxedo shirt. All three ended up on the floor like her bra and panties. With one hand, I grasped my undershirt from the back and pulled it over my head before letting it fall. Addison sat up and ran her hands from my shoulders, down the front of me until she reached the waist of my pants.

She gasped when after lowering my zipper, I eased the waistband down over my hips and my steel-hard cock sprung out. She leaned forward, circling the tip with her tongue, and I hissed. When she took me in her mouth, I groaned and wove my fingers in her hair. As often as I'd pleasured myself with my own hand, imagining her doing just this, I knew I wouldn't last if I let her continue. I took a step away and pushed her shoulders so she lay flat on her back. Without hesitating, I pulled her so her bottom was on the edge of the bed, spread her legs, and knelt between them.

Every whimper, every gasp, every moan drove me wild as I drank in her scent, her wetness.

I stood and grabbed a condom from the pocket of my pants, not being able to wait another minute to be inside her.

Addison's eyes were wide as she scooted back on the bed and watched me sheath my hardness. After settling back between her legs, I stroked her wetness with my cock before slowly easing the tip into her wet heat. My eyes rolled back in my head at how tight she felt.

I grabbed her ass, digging my fingers into her flesh, struggling to hold myself back from going in too deep, too hard. "Wrap your legs around me, baby."

I pushed in another inch, and she cried out. I looked into her eyes. "Am I hurting you?"

"God, no. I need more, Brix. Stop torturing me."

When I plunged the rest of the way in, Addison's fingernails dug into the flesh of my back. It was the most intoxicating pain I'd ever felt. I pounded hard, and she shattered, her legs tight around my waist, her pussy clenching my cock, and my name on her lips.

I slowed, gritting my teeth, trying to stave off my own release. Her eyes, wet with tears, darted back and forth between mine.

"Tell me whatever it is you're thinking, my precious, beautiful Addison."

"I...I've...never orgasmed like that. It was so... incredible. God, Brix."

I slowly rotated my hips, anxious to make her feel that way over and over again. I wanted—needed—to possess her, own her, make her mine forever. I wanted to hear her say she wanted to make me hers too. As I felt her heat clench me, only one refrain played in my head. I loved Addison Reagan with all my heart. I vowed that one day soon, she'd be able to trust in that, trust in me, and agree to be my wife.

"This is making love, baby. This is what I wanted for us," I said after bringing her to the precipice of pleasure and watching her float down from her orgasm for the third time.

With her legs still wrapped tightly around me, Addison rolled so our positions switched. With her hands firmly planted on my chest, she moved so I was barely inside her before taking me back in as deep as I could go. I closed my eyes, straining against taking over, but I wanted to feel this too much, knowing she was making love to me this time.

She stilled. "Brix, look at me."

I opened my eyes and let myself sink into the depths of everything I saw in hers.

"Addison, I…"

She shook her head. "Shh…just listen."

I tightened my grip on her waist, willing her to remain still and move at the same time.

"I love you, Gabriel Avila."

"Say it again."

She smiled. "I love you more than I ever dreamed possible." She moved then. Rotating her hips in a way that I couldn't hold back. I thrust my hips, slamming my cock into her.

We rolled to our sides, and with her leg draped over my hip, I jackhammered into her, shouting her name as the orgasm I'd denied myself overtook me.

32

Addison

"We can stay a few more nights if you'd like," Brix said over dinner on what was to be our last night sleeping in the tree house.

"A *few*?" I laughed, thinking about what our time here had already cost.

"Remember, I told you that if you'd let me, I'd keep our first date going for the rest of our lives."

I sighed. "At some point, we have to get back to those lives, Brix."

"Why?"

"Because we have *jobs*."

"Maybe it's time for me to take a step back from the winery operation at Los Cab."

I didn't know what to say. I couldn't imagine Brix not being the head winemaker for his family's business. I'd always thought the juice from their vineyards flowed through his blood.

"What will you do instead?"

He leaned forward. "You're going to think I'm crazy."

"Don't you mean *crazier*?"

"Probably, but here goes. I want to rebuild the Olallieberry Bakery and Diner."

"Yep, you're certifiable."

"Wanna hear why?"

Since he seemed so serious, I stopped teasing him. "I do."

"Because the best day I can remember is when you and I were there together."

"It was *one* day, Brix."

"I know, but I can't stop thinking about it."

"I'd say you have no idea how much work it is, but I'm sure running Los Cab is even more."

"We'd have our mothers' help."

I wasn't sure mine would want to go back. Maybe she'd consider it if Lucia agreed.

Admittedly, I was starting to miss the place. It was such a central part of the community. But working there and at Stave was exhausting. I wasn't sure how long I could keep it up.

"You're thinking about it, aren't you?"

"I'm thinking I don't know if I can go back to fifteen-hour days."

"I know you love Stave, but what if you cut back your hours or didn't work there at all?"

"I need to think about it, Brix."

"There's something else I want to run by you."

I sat back in my chair. The man had spent the last several hours overwhelming me in every way possible. He'd ravished my body, fed my spirit until I thought it would overflow, and challenged my mind with conversations like this one. "What?" I asked, wishing my voice didn't sound as tentative as it did.

"If we let Peg and my mom run the diner, you and I can spend more time at Tryst's ranch. I'd like to build a place of our own there."

My mind raced with what that might mean; I bluntly asked the first thing I thought of. "He wouldn't mind?"

"Definitely not." Brix always met my gaze when he talked, but that time, he looked away.

"There's something you're not telling me. Or don't want to."

He turned red, which made me smile. I loved that I could fluster Brix Avila since it was so rare that I'd ever seen him that way.

He sighed. "It's a surprise."

I studied him, realizing I'd never seen him as happy as he was right now. While he'd worked so hard to make all my dreams come true, there was something in the way he was talking that told me the surprise involved his own dreams. I'd never deny him that.

"I'm in."

"Wait. What did you say?"

"I'm *in*. You want to rebuild the diner? Do it. You want to build a place of your own on Tryst's ranch? Do it. You want to stop making wine? Do it. Whatever you want in life should be yours, Brix."

"I want to clarify a couple of things."

"All I'm saying is that you've worked so hard for as long as I've known you, and I'm sure long before that."

I stopped talking, but he didn't say anything.

"Sorry. Go ahead."

"I don't want to stop making wine."

"Okay."

"I don't want to build my own place on Tryst's ranch."

"But you just said—"

He shook his head. "I want to build *our* own place on the ranch. And as far as whatever I want in life being mine, there is one thing I want above everything else—to be with you." Brix put his hand under the table and pulled out a satin pouch. My eyes opened wide.

"Listen, I know I've done nothing but overwhelm you in the last several days, and while I should stop doing it, I don't want to. You said whatever I want should be mine, and I'm going to hold you to it." He pulled out a ring. "Be mine, Addison. Be my wife."

While a moment ago there were lively conversations taking place at every other table in the room, a hush had fallen as if everyone were holding their breath in the same way I was.

Was I ready for this? If Brix had waited days, weeks, months, or even years to propose, would my feelings for him ever change? I knew I wouldn't love him less, only more.

"I would love to be your wife, Brix."

Applause came from the other people in the restaurant before they returned to their previous conversations.

"It fits perfectly," I said as he slipped the solitaire diamond on my finger.

"We fit perfectly, baby."

33

Brix

As Addison and I drove down the coast, I thought about the conversation I had with my uncle the afternoon of the Wicked Winemakers' Ball. It was Tryst who'd convinced me not to wait to propose and who'd helped me pick out the ring Addison now wore.

"I have something to tell you too," he'd said on our drive back to Los Cab. "I've purchased the land adjacent to my ranch. It's another five thousand acres."

"Congratulations, Tryst. I know how much being there means to you. I can't wait to see what you do with the extra space. Soon, you'll have a village all your own."

"Not mine, nephew."

"You know what I mean."

"You do not know what I mean."

"Sorry, Tryst, but you lost me."

"The land I purchased is for you and Addison. You may tell her after you propose, or you may wait. Either way, it's a wedding present from me to the two of you."

I'd almost had to pull the truck off the road; I was so stunned. "That is a very generous gift. I don't know what to say."

"Ask me to help build you a house on the property."

"I would love it if you would."

"And be happy, Brix. As happy as your father and I were in our marriages."

"I plan to be."

Addison reached over and squeezed my hand. "You're deep in thought. Are you worried about what Ridge wants to talk to us about?"

He'd called shortly before we left our tree house hideaway and asked if we could swing by Seahorse when we returned to town. When I asked why, he said he'd explain when we got there.

I hated when he pulled shit like that, but I vowed not to let anything spoil my happiness today. Last night, Addison agreed to marry me; that was all I wanted to think about.

I kissed the back of her hand. "Not worried. I have the love of my life in the seat beside me. That's all that matters."

When I pulled through the gates of Seahorse, I saw several parked vehicles. It appeared all the members of Los Caballeros were here. I also saw Vader's car and hoped Peg might be here with him, making it the perfect opportunity to announce our engagement. I'd have to swear everyone to secrecy until we told my mother, though.

I opened the front door when the light above it went from red to green, happy to see both Peg and my mother were there. All of my brothers, even Cristobal, Sam, Alex, Maddox, and Coco had come too.

I'd planned to make our announcement after we had a chance to greet everyone, but when my mom's eyes lit up and her gaze focused on our clasped hands, I knew we couldn't wait.

"Addison and I are getting married!"

It was several minutes before I got to hold her hand again after we were surrounded by our friends and family offering their congratulations.

"We have another announcement," said Ridge, motioning for everyone to take a seat. We all did except for Press, Zin, and him.

Zin cleared his throat and took a piece of paper out of his pocket. "First, I asked Peg if I could share this with everyone, and I'm thrilled to say the insurance company has agreed to pay the claim on the diner, thus allowing her to pay off the mortgage on her house."

Addison hugged her mom, who was seated on the other side of her.

"And, as we anticipated, all charges have been dropped against Addison," Zin continued.

When his eyes met mine, I nodded and stood.

"I have another announcement."

My mother gasped and put her hands in front of her face. "Is Addy pregnant already?"

I shook my head and laughed when everyone else did. "No, Mama, but when she is, I'll be sure to let you know so you can be the one to make *that* announcement."

"Go ahead, Brix," said Ridge. "Tell us your real news."

"Addison and I have decided to rebuild the diner." I looked from Peg to my mother. "That's if we can talk the two of you into managing it for us."

In hindsight, I wondered if it would've been better to ask Peg privately rather than putting her on the spot, but when I saw her wide smile and eyes filled with tears before she hugged her daughter, I knew it was okay that I hadn't.

Kick and Snapper disappeared into Press' kitchen and returned with a tub filled with bottles of sparkling wine, which they proceeded to open.

"I'm really happy for you," said Ridge, coming to stand next to me by the windows that looked out over the Pacific Ocean.

"Thanks. I never dreamed life could be this good."

I turned to him, wondering if I'd see the same hurt I usually did when something made him think of how he'd once believed he had a chance with Alex, but I was pleased to see he didn't have that reaction.

"I wanted to give you an update on the prosecutor wanting to question Peg and Addy."

"Right. I'd forgotten all about that."

"That's what I was going to say—you can forget about it. She changed her mind."

"I don't care enough to ask why."

"You'll never change, Brix, and that doesn't bother me in the least." Ridge laughed and gripped my shoulder. "I'm heading out, but I'll catch up with you later this week."

After Ridge walked away, Zin joined me.

"Cru told me you asked him to set up a meeting with James Dunn from the Killeens."

"That's right. I intend to offer to pay off Murphy's debt. I don't want Addison or her mother to be in danger while we wait around for the FBI to act on their investigation."

"Give them until midweek."

I raised a brow. "Seriously?"

He smiled. "According to anonymous sources, something is about to go down, but keep that on the down low."

"Absolutely. Hey, do you know where Ridge is off to?"

Zin shook his head. "He said something about meeting with that damn prosecutor. Wouldn't tell me why either."

I shrugged. Just like I didn't care about why she'd changed her mind about questioning Peg or Addison, I didn't care why Ridge was meeting with her. If it had anything to do with me, he would've said so.

"You look happy," said Addison, coming up behind me and putting her arms around my waist.

"Thanks to you."

She rested her head against my back. "I love you, Brix, and I don't know how I'll ever thank you for everything you've done for me and my mom."

"Keep loving me, baby. That's all I'll ever need."

Epilogue

Brix

Six Months Later

Today was the grand reopening of the Olallieberry Bakery and Diner, and based on the line of people waiting to get in, we'd be breaking sales records within the first few hours.

Fortunately, Addison, Peg, my mom, and I had all the help we could ask for—and then some. Aunt Esmeralda and Alex were here along with Vader and Ridge. The rest of the *caballeros* had offered to help, but we were tripping over each other in the crowded kitchen as it was.

"Come with me, baby." I pulled Addison toward the back door and out to the place where we escaped to whenever we needed to talk or kiss. We did far more of the latter than the former.

After ravishing her mouth with mine, I squeezed her ass with both hands and pulled her closer to me. "You promised you wouldn't overdo it today, and I haven't seen you sit down once."

"I'm fine, Brix, I promise."

"How's the morning sickness?"

Addison looked at her watch. "As long as I eat again in the next fifteen minutes, I should be able to stave it off."

The first three months had been tough, but now that she was past the first trimester, it seemed like the nausea was easing up.

"Remember, I can run you home if you feel like you need to lie down." While we spent most of our time at the Los Cab house, I'd bought a little place right on the beach and less than a mile away so we didn't have to spend so much time commuting while the diner was being rebuilt.

"I don't want to miss a single minute of this day."

"Happy, Mrs. Avila?"

"More than I dreamed possible. What about you?"

"I'm in heaven."

I'd remained there from the moment Addison said she'd marry me, through to a month later when we said our vows in the temple on Tryst's ranch, to a month to the day after our wedding, when my beloved wife confirmed she was pregnant with our child. I had no doubt I'd feel that way for the rest of my life.

Now that the diner was open, I could focus more of my efforts on putting the finishing touches on the house on our ranch in Mexico, so once the baby was born, we could spend as much time there as Addison wanted to.

"It's a good life, isn't it, Brix?"

"I'd say it doesn't get any better than this, but every time I think that, you say or do something that proves me wrong."

"Do you think we could go back to the tree house again sometime?"

I smiled since I was one step ahead of her. "Tonight too soon?"

Keep reading for a preview of the next book in the Wicked Winemakers First Label Series, *Ridge's Release*

He's a charming billionaire winemaker with a broken heart. She's the assistant DA who's threatened to take Los Caballeros down. Will the upcoming WICKED WINEMAKER'S auction change everything?

RIDGE

I'm no stranger to getting what I want—until I was turned down by a woman I thought was mine. Now, that same woman has convinced me to participate in the annual bachelor auction. The one I tried to avoid, not realizing it was everything I needed. Determined to make the sassy DA see me in a new light, my greatest hope is to see how WICKED things can get between us…

SERAPHINA

I don't care how irresistible they are. The so-called good guys shouldn't be butting into our cases. This isn't a game of cops and robbers. This is real danger and real lives are on the line. When it's my sister's life that hangs in the balance, there's only one man who comes to mind, one man I know I can trust to save her. Somehow I know he'd climb to the top of any RIDGE to help me.

1

Ridge

From the window by the table, I had a perfect view of the restaurant's entrance as well as the ocean, volatile with today's storms.

I'd arrived early for my meeting with Seraphina Reeve, San Luis Obispo county's new assistant district attorney and the woman hell-bent on bringing an end to Los Caballeros—an organization whose traditions had withstood the tests of hundreds of years.

That she knew about the secret entity was a problem in itself. Did she truly, or like so many others, had she heard the rumors but had no confirmation?

Glancing up, I saw her walk through the front door, the look on her face as angry as the sea.

"Noah," she said, pulling out the chair on the opposite side of the table I'd chosen. "Not surprised you arrived before me." She, too, was early.

I waited for her to get settled. Even then, I didn't speak. She'd asked for this meeting, and I'd let her show her hand before I did mine.

"I see. Well, this is a waste of time," she muttered when I didn't offer up as much as a hello.

"Why did you ask for this meeting, Sera?"

Yeah, she hated when people called her that, but no one referred to me as Noah either, yet she insisted on doing so.

"As you know, your *club* has operated outside of the law for years. I'm here with an offer."

I raised a brow and waited.

"Brix Avila pleads guilty to several counts of obstruction of justice, and that will be the end of it. Along with proof that you've disbanded. If you or anyone else is found guilty of interfering with a single other investigation, we'll prosecute to the full extent of the law."

I took a minute to process the words she'd just vomited and did exactly what Brix would've done in my place. I sat back in my chair and laughed. Hard. Then signaled Barb, the waitress who usually waited on me.

"Check, please."

About the Author

USA Today Bestselling Author Heather Slade writes shamelessly sexy, edge-of-your seat romantic suspense.

She gave herself the gift of writing a book for her own birthday one year. Sixty-plus books later (and counting), she's having the time of her life.

The women Slade writes are self-confident, strong, with wills of their own, and hearts as big as the Colorado sky. The men are sublimely sexy, seductive alphas who rise to the challenge of capturing the sweet soul of a woman whose heart they'll hold in the palm of their hand forever. Add in a couple of neck-snapping twists and turns, a page-turning mystery, and a swoon-worthy HEA, and you'll be holding one of her books in your hands.

She loves to hear from her readers. You can contact her at heather@heatherslade.com

To keep up with her latest news and releases, please visit her website at www.heatherslade.com to sign up for her newsletter.

MORE FROM AUTHOR HEATHER SLADE

BUTLER RANCH
Kade's Worth
Brodie's Promise
Maddox's Truce
Naughton's Secret
Mercer's Vow
Kade's Return
Butler Ranch Christmas

WICKED WINEMAKERS
FIRST LABEL
Brix's Bid
Ridge's Release
Press' Passion
Zin's Sins
Tryst's Temptation

WICKED WINEMAKERS
SECOND LABEL
Beau's Beloved
Coming Soon:
Cru's Crush
Bones' Bliss
Snapper's Seduction
Kick's Kiss

ROARING FORK RANCH
Coming Soon:
Roaring Fork Wrangler
Roaring Fork Roughstock
Roaring Fork Rockstar
Roaring Fork Rooker
Roaring Fork Bridger

THE ROYAL AGENTS
OF MI6
Make Me Shiver
Drive Me Wilder
Feel My Pinch
Chase My Shadow
Find My Angel

K19 SECURITY
SOLUTIONS TEAM ONE
Razor's Edge
Gunner's Redemption
Mistletoe's Magic
Mantis' Desire
Dutch's Salvation

K19 SECURITY
SOLUTIONS TEAM TWO
Striker's Choice
Monk's Fire
Halo's Oath
Tackle's Honor
Onyx's Awakening

K19 SHADOW OPERATIONS
TEAM ONE
Code Name: Ranger
Code Name: Diesel
Code Name: Wasp
Code Name: Cowboy
Code Name: Mayhem

K19 ALLIED INTELLIGENCE
TEAM ONE
Code Name: Ares
Code Name: Cayman
Code Name: Poseidon
Code Name: Zeppelin
Code Name: Magnet

K19 ALLIED INTELLIGENCE
TEAM TWO
Code Name: Puck
Code Name: Michelangelo
Coming Soon:
Code Name: Typhon
Code Name: Hornet
Code Name: Reaper

PROTECTORS
UNDERCOVER
Undercover Agent
Undercover Emissary
Coming Soon:
Undercover Savior
Undercover Infidel
Undercover Assassin

THE INVINCIBLES
TEAM ONE
Code Name: Deck
Code Name: Edge
Code Name: Grinder
Code Name: Rile
Code Name: Smoke

THE INVINCIBLES
TEAM TWO
Code Name: Buck
Code Name: Irish
Code Name: Saint
Code Name: Hammer
Code Name: Rip

THE UNSTOPPABLES
TEAM ONE
Code Name: Fury
Code Name: Merried

COWBOYS OF
CRESTED BUTTE
A Cowboy Falls
A Cowboy's Dance
A Cowboy's Kiss
A Cowboy Stays
A Cowboy Wins

Made in United States
Troutdale, OR
03/02/2025